THE EQUESTRIENNE

THE EQUESTRIENNE

Uršuľa Kovalyk

Translated from the Slovak
by Julia Sherwood
and Peter Sherwood

Uršuľa Kovalyk is a poet, fiction writer, playwright and social worker. She was born in 1969 in Košice, eastern Slovakia, and currently lives in the capital, Bratislava. She has worked for a women's non-profit focusing on women's rights and currently works for the NGO Against the Current, which helps homeless people. She is the director of the Theatre With No Home, which works with homeless and disabled actors. She has published the short story collections, *Neverné ženy neznášajú vajíčka* (Unfaithful Women Lay No Eggs, 2002) and *Travesty šou* (*Travesty Show*, 2004), and two novels, *Žena zo sekáča* (*The Second-hand Woman*, 2008) and *Krasojazdkyňa* (*The Equestrienne*, originally published in Slovak in 2013 and in English by Parthian in 2016) which was shortlisted for Slovakia's most prestigious literary prize, the Anasoft Litera Award, and received the Bibliotéka Prize for 2013. Her most recent collection of short stories, *Čisté zviera* (*A Pure Animal*), appeared in 2018 and selected edition of her stories, *The Night Circus and Other Stories* was published in 2019.

Julia Sherwood was born and grew up in Bratislava, then Czechoslovakia. After studying at universities in Cologne and Munich she settled in the UK, where she spent more than twenty years working for Amnesty International. Since 2008 she has worked as a freelance translator. She lives in London and her joint translations from contemporary Slovak, Czech, and Polish prose with her husband Peter Sherwood include Peter Krištúfek's *Dom hluchého (The House of the Deaf Man)* for Parthian in 2014.

Peter Sherwood is a linguist and translator. He taught Hungarian language, linguistics and culture at universities in London and North Carolina for many years. He has translated the novels *The Book of Fathers* by Miklós Vámos and *The Finno-Ugrian Vampire* by Noémi Szécsi, as well as stories by Dezső Kosztolányi, Zsigmond Móricz, and others, along with works of poetry, drama, and philosophy.

http://juliaandpetersherwood.com

THE EQUESTRIENNE

Uršuľa Kovalyk

Translated from the Slovak

by Julia and Peter Sherwood

Parthian, Cardigan SA43 1ED
www.parthianbooks.com
The Equestrienne first published as *Krasojazdkyňa* in 2013
First published in 2016, Reprinted 2021

ISBN 978-1-913640-82-8
Editor: Susie Wild
Cover image by Lucia Dovičáková
Typeset by Elaine Sharples
Printed by 4edge Limited
Published with the financial support of the Welsh Books Council and the SLOLIA Committee, the Centre for Information on Literature in Bratislava, Slovakia
British Library Cataloguing in Publication Data
A cataloguing record for this book is available from the British Library.

THE EQUESTRIENNE

Uršuľa Kovalyk

I'm sitting on a broken bench not far from the paddock. It is late afternoon. The air is humid. There is a light drizzle. As if someone high above me decided to water geraniums with a sprinkler. Silence all round. Only a grey stallion in the paddock, his hard hooves kicking the ground. He is wild and bad-tempered. Every now and then he breaks into a canter, neighing furiously. He calls to his brothers who've been locked up in the cleaned-out stables for a long time. He is alone. I, too, am alone. I watch him, fully aware that he finds my presence irritating. Young stallions can't stand old women. I can't stand myself either. Drops of water sparkle on my liver-spotted hands. They look like transparent pearls cast before old swine. It was bound to happen. I'm relieved because I have finally made up my mind. It has taken me a long time though. I couldn't find the right one. All the horses seemed too tame. But then this hell-raiser of a stallion turned up. He was out of control. I knew he was my last chance. They are going to train him and break him in soon. And if he won't be tamed he'll be ground into salami. He doesn't know that yet. He looks at me imperiously, his flared nostrils inhaling the air mixed with my smell. I smell of urine. The stallion gives a loud snort and gallops to the far end of the paddock. Blue succory grows there in the summer. I've turned into succory myself. I've waited long enough for the succour that death will bring. But death is bloody stubborn. It wants to torment me. So I'll have to gatecrash, like an uninvited guest. So that the magnificent creature that's kicking up his rear out there takes me to you. I take a very deep breath to keep my fear in check. Slowly I approach the paddock. The stallion turns even wilder. He runs up and down in his fury. There is rage in his eyes. He is gorgeous. The epitome of untameable energy. He has magnificent muscles, powerful legs and a broad back. I approach him, and he backs away. He kicks the air menacingly. I clap my hands. He trots to the other end of the meadow. It takes me a while to shuffle over to him. My face is wet with rain, I feel exhausted and despondent. What if I fail? I pick up a stone and throw it at the stallion. He rears up, pawing the air with his hooves. I knew you could do it! I fling at him everything I can lay my hands on. Sticks, pine cones, clumps of wet grass. I goad him and egg him on, needle and mock him, stick my tongue out at him. I call him a coward. This is a duel. It's either him or me. I just hope he wins. Dusk is falling. The sky is steeped in a shimmering indigo. The stallion cavorts tempestuously. Grey foam covers his belly. He starts running at me as I walk towards him. I spit on him. That really enrages him. Fear makes my eyes bulge. I can hear someone whispering. Bits of silvery spider's webs float in the air. Suddenly my granny is sitting on the stallion's back. She looks at me with a kindly smile. I stop in my tracks. I peer into the animal's huge staring eyes. Rearing up, the stallion pummels my head with his hooves in slow motion. The pain knocks me out. My eyes fill with blood. I fall to the ground. I am rasping. The stallion comes at me again. Furiously, he tramples me. I can hear my bones crack. Unbearable pain makes my tongue spill out of my mouth. I'm gagging and choking at the same time. It lasts an eternity. Everything seems so distant now. I feel calm. My battered body dissolves into phosphorescent blue particles. Slowly they rise towards the sky. Like steaming soup on Sundays. Granny strokes my face tenderly. I'm floating in the air and the meadow looks smaller and smaller. I don't feel anything now. The grey stallion's shadow circles around me. His rain-soaked tail begins to summon up images from my fading memory.

I remember everything. The darkly pounding heart. The warm liquid that rocked me to the rhythm of her steps. The red light shining through the belly tissue, tickling my still undeveloped eyes as I floated in amniotic fluid, attaching myself to the wall of the womb from time to time. Like a bristlenose catfish in an aquarium. My mum giggled and a few drops of urine trickled into her knickers. I remember it so well. The feeling of total security and perfect harmony. The gentle rocking, the muffled noises. The amniotic fluid tasting of oranges. We were linked by the umbilical cord. The most perfect communication channel in the universe.

I had a responsible mother. She didn't light up once throughout the nine months. And so I grew. Buried in my warm cave I waited for the astral clock to tick my time away. Too many flies had hatched that summer and I could hear their gentle buzzing from inside her belly. Suddenly the womb began to sway. Enormous pressure started to push me out of my nest. That was the first time I felt fear. The womb squeezed me, forcing me to slide down a narrow, slimy tunnel. I resisted at first but then I felt that my mother couldn't wait any longer for me to leave her belly. I realised there was no going back. So I pushed the tunnel open with my head and emerged into a sizzling hot day.

I registered everything. The white tiles, the doctor's tired look. 'It's a girl', came his laconic announcement. He patted my bottom and handed me to a woman standing next to him.

I started to cry. The air, reeking of disinfectant, painfully distended my lungs. The nurse checked that everything was as it should be. She gave me a wash. Weighed me, measured me and swaddled me. I was ready. Perfectly developed. Well made. Capable of surviving here, on this planet. Then the nurse put me down on a white breast. It smelled delicious. I latched on and started sucking greedily. I felt the sweetish taste of milk on my tongue. I stared and drank. A huge flesh fly sitting on the nurse's blue and white uniform was calmly wiping its legs.

Some time later I was transferred to a white cage. I lay there all swaddled up. Lonely. Without the familiar heartbeat. Nothing but crying. Somebody's arms would move me to a battered white trolley and carry me over to the breast. That was my world. The breast, the nipple, the milk. Mum's mouth opened, she bared her teeth. Her eyes with their broken veins and her moist lips on my head. Her unique smell. My empty brain registered scraps of the world. And so I slept and suckled. Emptied my bowels. Screamed. One day my mum wrapped me in a yellow blanket, carried me out into the blinding light and put me in a pram. A bug-eyed red parrot swayed frenziedly above my head. It made me dizzy. After a long time I was put into a cage again.

A face leaned down towards me. A smiling face. It smelled of garlic. It said: 'Just look at those huge eyes!' That was how I met my granny.

I was put to sleep in a cot with a cuddly teddy bear. I was just a helpless little animal. Unable to move. I had no control over my arms and legs. And that voice of mine! It was so grating! The expression on the teddy bear's face was numb. I was happy to see real human faces bend over me. One was framed by jet-black hair and had big, blue smiling eyes. That was my mum. She smelled of milk. 'What a sweetie you are,' she cooed.

The other, the one bending over me, had flaxen hair and long dark lines above her eyes. That was my granny. Only later did I learn that the lines represented eyebrows drawn on with cheap eyeliner from the chemist's.

I got over the first children's illnesses and finally began to understand human speech.

'Now the fun can start,' Granny said. 'Looks like something's stirring in that little brain,' she shouted from the kitchen as she strained her homemade noodles.

I was sitting on the potty pecking at a roll and repeating the words 'little brain' over and over again, trying to pronounce them properly.

Mum was combing her hair in the bathroom. She was going out to a party now that she'd finally weaned me. She had met a nice uncle, apparently. Granny warned her to watch out, 'those divorced guys could be real bastards'. Mum just told her off for swearing in front of me.

Granny ran out of the kitchen waving the pasta strainer and screaming: '*Drágám*, my dear, nobody is going to tell me what to do in my own house!' No one in my family swore as much as she did. She had a theory that it was healthy to swear freely and as long as she did it at home it was no one else's business. She claimed that not being able to swear properly was as bad as not being able to take a dump. Constipation would kill you sooner or later. Granny was half-Hungarian and needed to let her hot blood out from time to time, to give it a good airing, as she used to say. And because she and Mum often had huge rows, I picked up the worst Hungarian swearwords you can imagine.

I was two by the time I started to walk. All the other kids were already tottering around the sandpit. I was crawling like a crocodile, licking the dirty floor clean. Granny used to say I was weedy and must have inherited some disease. From my father. They took me to see a doctor but he couldn't find anything wrong with me. He said my development might be slightly delayed and they should just give it time. So they did. They tied a long rope around my feet and attached the other end to a bench so I could crawl around in an endless circle. Now Mum could enjoy her coffee in peace without having to chase after her child like other parents. And so for a long time my most frequent companions were firebugs. They desperately tried to get away from my fingers. I remember one particular afternoon. A fierce wind was blowing. Plastic bags from an overturned rubbish bin flapped about, Granny was drinking her coffee and Mum was chain-smoking. I stood up and slowly took my first, shaky steps. The wind was behind me, forcing me to walk faster and faster. My baby windcheater ballooned like a sailing boat and I took off.

'She's walking!' Mum yelled, flinging her cigarette away.

'Bullshit! She's flying!' Granny countered and went to help Mum catch the flying child.

I don't know who my father was. I'm not sure Mum knew either. I never knew my grandpa. I had no brothers or uncles. Males didn't really figure in my family. The only males we would see were visitors. Like the neighbour who lived on the fifth floor. He used to come and play rummy at our flat. Once I had learned to talk and my little brain was working at full throttle I asked about my grandpa. Smiling mysteriously, Granny took out a photo from a drawer. It showed a tall gentleman with a black pencil moustache. His hair was greased down. He was holding a hat in his hand. A young woman with two lines for eyebrows was on his arm. She was also wearing a hat. Hers was decorated with beautiful flowers. Granny said my grandpa was a great looker and an even greater whoremonger.

'So where is he now?' I asked.

Granny took me by the hand. She opened the wardrobe and took out some kind of a container hidden behind her coats. 'Here!'

I stared at the container for a long time but Granny didn't let me open it.

'We must let Grandpa rest,' she said with a sigh, putting him back behind some old lace redolent of mothballs.

Later that night, when I went to bed, I imagined a tiny little gentleman in a hat snoring in the urn in a tiny little bed.

Our life was full of fun. Granny spent most of her time cooking, playing cards with neighbours, drinking *barackpálinka,* the Hungarian apricot brandy, and finding fault with Mum. She used to say Mum had a clitoris for a brain. I pictured a beautiful flower inside her head. A kind of gladiolus. Every time they played cards they ended up fighting furiously because Granny was cheating. Then she would have a shot of *pálinka*, start swearing and stay up late singing Hungarian songs.

Miskolc smelled of apricots in the summertime when we visited Granny's three aunties in Hungary. They were Aunts Márta *néni*, Juci *néni* and Erzsébet, whom we all called *keresztmama*, godmother. They were former teachers who had been banned from teaching. Because they were said to have an insufficiently positive attitude to the socialist system. They lived in a run-down art nouveau townhouse with an outside toilet. The water heater made a frightening noise in the bathroom, which had bluish-green mould growing on the walls and the fattest spiders running around that I'd ever seen. Although town gas had been installed in their flat after the war, *keresztmama* would light a fire every morning and only ever cook on the stove. We understood each other perfectly even though I couldn't speak a word of Hungarian. They called me *drága gyerek*, dear child, and stuffed me with the most delicious Hungarian salamis.

I loved the old, mouldy house full of magnificent antique furniture. It belonged to Juci *néni*. She was a countess. A real one. She had grown up in an enormous mansion. When the commies took it away, she was left with just a few pieces of furniture and a stunning glass-fronted cabinet filled with precious china statuettes. Ancient dollies, puppies with emerald eyes, silver umbrellas, pouting babies, tiny majolica pitchers and faïence apples. Knick-knacks her suitors had given her on her birthdays. Every time we came to visit I felt like I was in a castle. The aunts never married. They didn't have boyfriends or children. They had been brought together by the war and later by the totalitarian regime.

Márta *néni* was a placid, chubby matron with dirty fingernails. Her favourite occupation was lounging in bed and reading. She sported a little moustache on her upper lip. She shaved it every second day with a razor. She used to show me old storybooks with wonderful illustrations. Sometimes she would read to me and the magic sound of words I didn't understand would lull me to sleep.

Juci *néni* looked like a young girl grown old. Her snow-white hair was held back with a beautiful mother-of-pearl hair slide. She liked to listen to political broadcasts on the radio, graciously dusting wardrobes with a velvet duster. Before lunch she would have a shot of *Becherovka* liqueur and she insisted on three-course lunches every day. She would not get into any horseplay with me. She would just stroke my head from time to time and say, '*intelligens gyerek!*', clever child. On rainy days she would play a record of the actor Zoltán Latinovits reciting Hungarian poetry. His sonorous voice darted around the vast flat like an invisible dragonfly. I danced to the rhythm of his words although their meaning escaped me. *Keresztmama* spent all day fussing about in the kitchen. When she laughed, she banged her fist on the table. She used to give me juicy smackers on the cheeks. She wore her waist-length black hair tied in a thick plait that bobbed about in the chicken soup vapour. Chicken feet poked out of the pot. Floating elegantly among bits of vegetables, they reminded me of synchronised swimmers. *Keresztmama* would prod them with a fork at regular intervals.

We went to visit them every summer. Just Granny and I. Without Mum. They would make up my bed in the guest room where an enormous tapestry covered a whole wall. It showed a shepherdess with a bunch of sheep that looked rather like dogs. I used to go to sleep in a real countess's bed!

Granny and I spent whole days at the Tapolca baths. She had set her mind on whipping my weedy body into shape by forcing me to swim. There were several huge swimming pools, stalls selling *lángos,* fried flat bread, and hordes of kids. The entire communist bloc must have been represented. I stood at the edge of the pool. My shoulder blades stuck out so far they almost pierced the whipped-cream clouds.

'Jump!' Granny shouted.

I looked first at her, then the water, then back at her. She hadn't painted on her eyebrows that morning and there was something sadistic about her expression. I reminded her that I couldn't swim.

'Every girl can swim,' she hollered. 'You just have to find it in yourself. Go on, don't be scared. Jump in!'

I couldn't believe she was serious. I don't think anyone thought she was serious. They were all staring at us and I saw concern in people's eyes. A little girl from Dresden sitting on a chequered rug stopped chewing her pancake. I had no choice. I couldn't disappoint Granny. I took a deep breath and plunged in. The water closed above me. I knew I was sinking to the bottom. Panic took hold. My neck muscles tensed. Cramp twisted my legs. Air bubbles danced madly around my face. It occurred to me that this was how a cherry must feel in the lemonade *keresztmama* used to serve with lunch. I wanted to swim upwards but an invisible stone tied to my legs dragged me back down. I was suffocating. An air bubble in my ears went plop. I opened my eyes underwater. I saw someone's yellow and white legs kicking out, a striped swimming costume dancing and a pair of blue flippers moving. I summoned all my remaining strength. I started thrashing about. To my surprise an invisible force lifted me up to the surface and I could finally catch my breath. My eyes stung.

'About time!' shouted Granny and said something to the lifeguard. He looked scared.

I wriggled and kicked and splashed about. Like a fish struck by electric current. My eyes popping, I struggled to the edge of the pool. As I scrambled out, breathless, Granny looked around with pride. Somebody said something in German. The little girl on the rug finished off her pancake.

Something weird must have happened to my brain. I began to see strange things in other people. As I looked at Granny standing in the *lángos* queue, I suddenly saw another figure inside hers. Within the plump outlines of her physical body there was another, transparent one. It was the body of an old Native American squaw with a turquoise amulet around her neck. Granny turned to me with a question but I couldn't take in what she said. All I could see was the wrinkled face of the squaw with her blazing eyes. 'There's an Indian woman inside you,' I said. Granny waved her hand dismissively.

That evening I dozed off in an armchair while Granny and the aunties played rummy for forints, drinking cherry *pálinka* and laughing their heads off.

'*Már alszik*', she's fallen asleep, *keresztmama* whispered, and carried me to bed.

A horse and cart passed by the window and the monotonous clip-clopping of the horses' hooves put me into a deep sleep. I woke up in the middle of the night. I was thirsty. My back was sore from the sun. I climbed out of bed. The door of the aunties' bedroom was open. In the dim light streaming in from the street through the window I saw three young naked women lying in a huge bed. They were snogging and fondling each other with their long plaited hair. In the silence that reigned I heard Granny snoring. The women touched each other's necks and collarbones. They kissed each other on the thighs, lifting each other's firm breasts with their white hands. Gently but passionately. Their alabaster bodies intertwined. I stood there watching the spectacle for a long time. I even forgot to have my drink. In the morning I tried to see the alabaster woman inside the plump Márta *néni*. She was snacking on lard. But however hard I examined her face I could see nothing but fresh stubble. Márta *néni* gave me a cheerful wink and licked her greasy fingers.

I thought it would pass. But it didn't. In time I learned how to bring on this state myself. I just had to lower my chin, as if about to rest it on the top of my chest, and roll my eyes to the back of my head. At first it hurt but after a while my eye muscles got used to it. I would often look at people this way. Mum, for example. She was sprawled out in front of the TV, wrapped in a thick bathrobe. The flickering light from the TV screen turned her face blue, and what I saw on the sofa was an Indian princess, with intricate henna patterns on her body and a golden nose-ring. She wiggled her thighs as she fondled her pussy. Inside my nursery school teacher there was hidden a wheezing nun, while inside our family doctor I found a boy sticking his tongue out. Some people had just a grey stone inside them. I also came across people with dead fish floating about in them. I was only sorry that I couldn't look inside myself and find out who was lurking there. The trick just didn't work in front of the mirror.

And so I grew older, went to nursery school and spent summers visiting my aunties. I was still very sickly. I was liable to trip even when walking on level ground. By now Granny had given up on raising me to be a sportswoman. Mum's job involved some travel. Sometimes she was away from home for a whole week. And so Granny and I had to manage on our own. We would get up to all sorts of mischief. We would rub hot chilli peppers onto toilet paper, a rare commodity in those days. Then we placed the roll in a plastic bag and left it hanging on the door to our flat. Gleefully, Granny waited for the neighbour to pinch it. He was a thief and getting a burning hot arse would teach him a lesson! I put a lot of effort into rubbing the loo paper.

Granny liked to crack jokes. If I happened to stand in front of a switched-on TV, she would ask if my dad had been a glass blower. She idolised Géza Hofi, the Hungarian comic who dared to mock all the world's comrades. Sometimes he ended up in prison and would vanish from the TV screen for long periods. That drove Granny mad. She would bang pots and plates in the kitchen and curse the 'fucking proles' for putting talented artists behind bars. She wasn't afraid of anything.

She never went anywhere without a real knife. A tiny silver flick-knife it was. 'All the women in our family carry knives,' she whispered. 'One day you'll get one too.' I asked what I might need a knife for. Granny explained that it was the only thing that worked with lechers. She passed the blade a hair's breadth away from her neck with a swish. I should always look whatever scared me most right in the eye. And I would no longer be afraid.

The thing that scared me most was the cellar of our tenement. It was dark, stank of cat piss and the lights were always out. The thieving neighbour had stolen the light bulbs. Some of the dividing walls had been torn down, creating cave-like alcoves. In my imagination they were home to some disgusting slimy creatures. Child gobblers! I told Granny about them. One evening she made me go down with her. I squealed and begged her to let me go back home but she shone her torch into the most horrible nooks, saying: 'Look, there's nothing in there. Only big fat spiders.'

I adored her. She was so strong. I loved Mum as well, but in a different way. Mum was beautiful, fragrant and hardly ever at home. We saw each other in bed in the mornings. She would wake me up to go to nursery school and I would kiss her, fondling her firm, warm breasts. I couldn't get enough of them. Every now and then I dreamt of latching on to her nipples. But she wouldn't let me. She said I was too old now, that she would miss her bus and get into trouble at work.

Granny loved to tell stories. Tales of war and the like. After the war the commies had taken away the tavern she and grandpa used to own. Greedy bastards, she called them. Their tavern was famous for its homemade ham hock, delicious chicken *paprikás* and exquisite wines. It was a place where big business deals were clinched. But one day someone daubed the word 'bourgeois' on the door in black paint. From then on things went downhill very fast. Soldiers arrived and all my grandparents were allowed to take with them was their clothes, some bedding and a few bits and pieces. They became paupers. She said

Grandpa had wept. And these same greedy bastards had robbed Juci *néni* and *keresztmama* in Hungary. 'Don't you ever forget that, my child!' she used to say. In the afternoons at nursery school when we were supposed to have our nap, I would daydream. I would imagine saving Granny from the greedy bastards, stabbing their bellies with a long knife.

I had no friends. We lived in a block full of pensioners. In nursery school I wasn't popular with the other kids. I preferred to play on my own anyway. I was bored by all the rope skipping, scrambling on climbing frames and playing tag. My movements were awkward and uncoordinated. I was bullied. Our comrade teachers had pat explanations for everything. There was no baby Jesus, Santa Claus was just the school cleaner in fancy dress and those who didn't learn a poem about Lenin by heart wouldn't be allowed to join the Sparkies and, later on, the Young Pioneers. 'Who cares?' I blurted out. In a tragic voice the teacher declared that I would never get to university and that I had no idea what she was talking about. One day a boy assaulted me. He grabbed me by the hair and started punching me in the stomach. My first reaction was fear. But then I remembered what Granny had said and bashed him on the nose with a toy tank. The teacher complained to Granny and said I was an aggressive little bruiser. That's what she should tell the nasty little wretch who had hit me in the belly, Granny replied.

The cold spring had me totally fooled. A jagged sun shone outside the window giving the illusion of hot summer. Tricked by the sun's rays I ran out just in knee-high socks. I promptly caught a cold, which developed into a throat infection. My tonsils looked like red scoops of raspberry ice cream. Granny put a duck-fat compress on my throat and sat down by my bed. She stroked my hair for a while. Then she handed me a long cream-coloured box. 'This is for you,' she said.

I opened the box clumsily. There, on a bedding of soft satin, rested a beautiful knife. A picture of a wolf with bared teeth was engraved on its mother-of-pearl handle. Granny sighed and went back to the kitchen. I stayed in bed, playing with my dolls. I cut their hair off with the knife pretending they had caught some strange disease. Suddenly I felt someone's kiss. It was Granny's old squaw. Her turquoise amulet gently brushed my hair. She said she had to go now. I told the dolls scattered on the duvet to keep their mouths shut and went to the kitchen. I found Granny lying on the floor. She was staring at the ceiling, open-mouthed. I touched her. It felt strange. She reminded me of meat on a butcher's counter. The Indian squaw stood beside her body, fixing me with her eyes and telling me she wasn't able to leave. I took off my pyjamas. To this day I don't know what gave me the idea. I unbuttoned Granny's blouse and lay down on top of her. The Indian woman sang a song. I lay on top of Granny's body for hours feeling it slowly going cold. The squaw's song started to fade away. By early evening it had disappeared completely. Then she vanished. I got up, put my clothes back on and waited for Mum to come home from work. It was a long wait. It was very late and I was half asleep by the time I heard the rattling of her keys in the door. Mum turned on the light and I said 'Granny has died on us, you should make us some dinner.'

So there was a funeral to attend. It was held at a crematorium with two weeping sculptures instead of columns. The whole place was sombre. Even the squirrels frolicking on the hundred-year-old pines had tears in their eyes. We said our last farewells to Granny, who had been laid out in a coffin dressed in her favourite dress and with a book in her hands. She looked contented. Her face bore that familiar otherworldly expression. I realised that something wasn't quite right. I fished out some eyeliner from Mum's bag and drew two thin lines on Granny's forehead where her eyebrows used to be. A man gestured for the coffin to be closed. The Hungarian song *Szomorú vasárnap*, 'Gloomy Sunday', came from the speakers. The coffin glided solemnly towards an enormous furnace. The furnace opened its jaw and swallowed her like a little canapé, about to turn into grey ashes the woman I had snuggled up to so many times. Mum was beside herself. She was wailing. Snot streamed from her nose. I tried to comfort her. I told her how the Indian squaw sang to me and then flew up to heaven. When it was all over we went to a restaurant for a drink. Mum ordered some cherry *pálinka* and, exceptionally, I was allowed to have a glass of *kofola*! Nursery school kids were not normally allowed to drink Czechoslovakia's answer to Coke but a funeral was a special occasion. Mum stopped crying. She downed one shot of *pálinka* after another until she fell asleep with her head on the table. The waiter called us a taxi and helped us into it. A tall man, he supported Mum gently and said to me: 'When you get home, wake up your sister so she can pay the driver.'

Now we had two little urns, solemnly stored in an antique dresser. I used to pick them up and tell them all our news. Mum sorted out Granny's wardrobe and threw out all sorts of odds and ends: old torn nylons, curlers and hairnets, spectacle cases. She gave all of Granny's clothes to our ground-floor neighbour. Every time I saw the woman wearing Granny's floral dress my heart ached. Our flat was strangely silent without Hungarian swear words and songs ringing through it. Mum had nobody to fight and play cards with into the small hours. She could no longer go to the cinema with her boyfriends because she had to do the laundry, look after me and cook our meals. We would look at each other, think of Granny and burst into tears.

'It'll pass,' Mum said, pouring herself a glass of wine.

I had to stay in the nursery school until later every day. Mum worked until four, which meant that I was among the last to leave. Whenever she missed her bus, comrade teacher would take me home with her. A beautiful ancient clock in her dining room chimed its ding-dang-dong every hour on the hour and I knew I'd been there for a very long time. Mum felt very guilty. She would turn up, out of breath, and press me to her wet coat. She apologised, blaming her boss, that idiot who wouldn't let her leave on time.

The teacher said sternly: 'What will you do once Karolína starts school? And besides, the child needs a dad.'

And so Mum decided to try and find me a daddy. I drew a picture of him on a piece of paper. I showed it to Mum but she said I'd drawn a picture of Granny.

'But I want a dad just like that,' I replied, stamping my foot and glowering at her. I didn't make life easy for her.

Not only was I given to fits of temper, but to make things worse, the greedy bastards took our flat away. It was one of those small-scale flats that used to be allocated to pensioners. But our pensioner was no longer with us. Mum filled out some forms at work so that we would have somewhere to live. We packed our stuff, furniture, urns and all, and moved to a new housing estate still under construction on the fringes of the city.

I remember the day as if it were yesterday. A van loaded with our furniture stopped outside a high-rise block of flats. The driver plonked me down in the street and began unloading the crates with his assistant while I stood on the pavement. There was mud everywhere and nothing to be seen but identical grey prefab buildings. Not a single tree, playground or shop. Only empty cans scattered about, battered Portakabins and a vast water-filled pothole with miserably croaking frogs. I glanced at Mum to check that this was for real. Maybe she would start swearing in Hungarian. Maybe she'd make the driver turn round and drive us back to our old flat that still smelled of Granny. But instead she said: 'We'll be fine, don't worry!' and shoved a bag into my hand. The lift wasn't yet working. Slowly I trundled up to the fifth floor listening to the men grumble as they hauled the old dresser up the narrow stairs. Mum got cross and told them not to piss her off because there was a child around.

Once everything had been brought inside, Mum paid the men and closed the door. I walked around the empty flat, which looked like an eggshell. Two tiny rooms, a corridor, a kitchen, a Formica bathroom. The toilet didn't flush. We had to pour buckets of water down the bowl the whole weekend. Mum said I could choose the colour for the walls in my room. I chose orange. It reminded me of the apricots I used to eat in Miskolc. That was how our life on the new estate began. The umbilical cord that tied us to Granny even after her death was severed for good.

Soon after the move I started school. In an unsightly, grey building full of chilly classrooms. Bulldozer tyres had left enormous potholes in the playground. When it rained they filled with water. We used to catch tadpoles in them. They trembled all the time as if they'd caught a chill. As more families with children moved to the estate the school gradually filled up. It started to come to life. There were thirty of us in my form. Thirty scoundrels, as the teacher used to say. Thirty unruly brats, girls and boys, interested in everything except learning. I didn't like school. Not a bit. All those socialist greetings. Unbearable. My favourite occupation was staring out of the huge, badly-insulated windows. I watched the white clouds drifting by and found in them faces of people, ogres, sometimes animals. Flocks of black crows flew all around. Sometimes I would spot a shrieking falcon, preparing to swoop down on a rat. When the wind blew it made the windowpanes rattle, playing a tune that made me want to dance. The teacher told me off, she sent notes to my mum and tried to engage my attention with something interesting. A skeleton in the science room or a chicken embryo in formaldehyde. But I was interested in the life on the other side of the window, not in corpses. It took me ages to learn to write and Mum had to spend hours helping me with my homework. I would mix up the letters of the alphabet and was bored of copying them out over and over again. Somehow I scraped through from one year to the next.

At some point they made our form the school swimming team. We got a new form teacher, the most charming bitch I'd ever met. All sweetness and light when dealing with our parents and the devil incarnate with us kids. The minute the door closed on the last parent her face would contort into a cruel grin. Her eyes would narrow to two hate-filled slits. She would let out a scream and a hiss, and slam a long ruler down on the desk. She also used to beat us with that ruler, hitting us on our backs, hands, and heads to hammer our times tables and the Young Pioneer's oath into us. With every stroke of the ruler she would pummel another rule into our heads, convinced that she had made us wiser. Wiser through another beating. She scared us out of our wits and many kids would be sick before her class. She used to march up and down between the desks checking our posture, making sure we had our hands behind our backs, that our satchels were properly hung up and the pencils in our pencil cases properly sharpened. I could smell her body odour. She reeked of rotting flesh sprinkled with a nasty sweet perfume. It made me nauseous. Her 'fragrance' scared me even more. It made me want to run away, smash my head through the window and fly off. But I just sat there horror-struck and paralysed. I decided to try my eye trick on the teacher. When I looked inside her I saw a haggard policewoman wielding a baton. She bared a gold tooth in a sinister grin, waved her baton and yelled: 'I will turn you into human beings!' Honestly, there are some souls that should never have come into this world.

School was my Hell Number One, and swimming practice was Hell Number Two. I wasn't able to keep up with my classmates. I couldn't learn even the simplest strokes. I just about managed to keep afloat but I was a total mess. I spun around my own axis flailing my arms as if about to drown any minute. My classmates would laugh their heads off. After endless hours of torture the coach decided it made more sense to let me sit it out on the bench. I was hopeless. A simple front flip was an acrobatic feat quite beyond me. My arm muscles weren't strong enough to hold on to the safety rings. I plopped down like a rotten pear and ended up with an F in a subject any idiot could master. Even worse, Mum seemed quite serious about finding me a daddy. She started to bring male visitors home at night. I was already in bed, and would hear a gentle knock on the door, followed by hushed laughter and whispers. The smell of men seeped into my bedroom. I knew what went on behind the closed door of Mum's room. The moaning and shrieking repelled me. I was terribly jealous. The thought of a man touching Mum's body sent me into an uncontrollable rage. I was livid and would sob through the nights, imprisoned in my helplessness. I learned to hate. Mum introduced me to some of her boyfriends. One of them had a hoarse voice and a thick beard. He shook my hand limply as he ogled Mum's breasts. Why waste time on a weedy kid. I was plain, scrawny, with hands covered in eczema and big ears sticking out through my badly cut hair. I was no Lolita promising future sexual delights. Just a disgusting little brat in the way of a stud on heat. I would sit quietly in the living room stuffing myself with salt sticks as I watched the two grown-ups billing and cooing. The nose-ringed Indian princess fondled her pussy. Its scent hit the guy's nostrils, clouding his brain and making him forget all about my existence.

And so I chose to drift about outside. I'd hang around the department store staring at black peppermint liquorice sticks, at the bus stop where I'd pick up any loose change, in a bar where *kofola* was served on draught. I started to loiter about after school. Mum was either at work or on a date. Our home became a dark, empty cage. Gradually, as the housing estate grew, I would wander around exploring its nooks and crannies. Unfinished blocks of flats, garages, rusty climbing frames without a coat of paint. I would climb huge hills of soil that had been dumped there for no obvious reason and wade through chocolate-coloured puddles in holes left by excavators. The first, slightly twisted stalks of coltsfoot shot up along the kerb, attracted by the early spring sun. The wind blew in dust mixed with cement from the building site, charging my hair with electricity in the arid air.

At the school canteen they gave us pig's lungs in white sauce for lunch. The unbearable stench trailed the whole length of the school corridor. I decided to skip lunch and ran home. I was so desperate for a pee that I undid my trousers in the lift. I rushed into our flat, only to find Mum and the bearded guy at the washbasin in the bathroom. I stopped in my tracks, as if someone had poured boiling water over me, my trousers at half mast. Mum was naked and she was holding the bearded guy's purple sausage in her hand, sticking it between her legs. I wet myself. My throat clenched with embarrassment. I couldn't breathe. I stood there for a moment trying to catch my breath and felt my face going red. The bearded guy's sausage wilted in Mum's hands. I ran away, locked myself in my room and bawled into my pillow. Mum shot out of the bathroom. She called my name. She knocked on the door. The guy told her to calm down, not to be hysterical. I was a big girl and this was all part of life, after all. I was a hypersensitive kid and she ought to be stricter with me. The smoke from Mum's ciggie stung my nose. Standing behind the door she babbled something about love and why wasn't I at school. She rambled on about family, a nice good daddy, nice little girls and trips to the seaside. Finally they cleared off. I felt sick. I stood in front of the mirror. My swollen face was covered in snot. I felt dirty. Disgusted with myself. Disgusted with Mum and her lover.

I had to do something fast. And so I ran away from home. I walked fast. I got to the far end of the estate. I passed the last garages, car repair shops and the dusty magnesite processing plant. I reached the outskirts where a faded city limit sign shone white by the roadside. I kept going, determined to go to the very end of the world. Somewhere I wouldn't have to see a naked Mum or that purple sausage. I ran out into a field. Clumps of the freshly-ploughed soil looked like the backs of dolphins leaping out of the sea. The wind was fragrant with the smell of dug-up dirt and my presence startled a pheasant. The field seemed endless. My lungs finally opened up in the fresh air and I was able to breathe again. I unzipped my windcheater. Rays of sunshine fell upon the ground through tattered clouds like yellow straws in a glass of lemonade. I followed a path across the field towards some tall pine trees, up to a patch covered with wild garlic. The forest smelled of freshly toasted bread. It was watching me with its invisible eyes. I felt thousands peering at me from tree branches and dark animal burrows. A couple of frightened wood pigeons flapped their wings and disturbed a black-and-white magpie. With a blood-curdling squawk it disappeared into the fog rising above the treetops. I trod gingerly. The immense silence settling on the moss calmed my nerves. I found myself near a vast paddock.

There was a girl standing there. She was leaning over the fence trying to attract the attention of a fat grey horse. The animal looked at her impassively, chewing on something. 'Come on, Sesil, I've got a nice carrot for you! Come over here!' she said, leaning down so far that she nearly fell over the other side of the fence. '

'Looks like he's too full,' I piped up.

The girl gave a start and turned to face me. She had a huge strip of plaster on her face. She grinned, her green eyes blinking: 'Sesil too full? That'll be the day! This greedy creature can never get enough!' As she said this, the horse moved closer and gently took the carrot from her hand into its soft black lips.

Her name was Romana. She was a year older than me. She lived somewhere at the other end of town. She had a limp, as her right leg was slightly shorter than her left. She said one day her mum was going to buy her special shoes with built-up heels. Then both her legs would be the same length. Romana showed me around the riding centre. She knew all the horses by name. She was a bubbly and fearless girl, not scared to climb into the fiercest stallion's box. Lombard the stallion kicked out and bared its teeth at us.

Romana spent a lot of time at the riding centre. Like me, she hated school and things were really bad at home. 'My dad drinks,' she whispered and looked around to make sure nobody could hear.

She was desperate to ride but the riders were too stuck up. None of them would let her ride their horse. So she tried her luck with fat Sesil in the paddock.

'Aren't you scared you'll fall off?' I asked.

She took me by the hand and dragged me towards Sesil, limping. She patted him, and deftly leapt on his back. 'It's easy, see? You just have to relax your spine,' she instructed me. Sesil strode about lazily, his hooves clopping on the hardened soil. Romana stretched and twisted, assuming a variety of positions on his back. She even lay down and pretended to be asleep. I wanted to have a go, too. But then I remembered how weedy I was, and gave up: 'I'm hopeless. I'll just fall off.'

Romana laughed but I didn't mind at all.

'If a cripple like me can do it, you can do it with both hands tied behind your back!' She jumped off and stretched out. 'Chop-chop. I'll show you,' she said and I was too weak to resist.

Somehow I managed to scramble onto Sesil's back. Suddenly I was much taller. The horse was walking. Very slowly. It made me feel dignified and important. I could feel his large, warm body and calm movements. I caressed his muscular neck and let my legs dangle.

'So, how does it feel?'

'Wonderful!' I shouted enthusiastically. Then I lay down on Sesil's comfortable, almost-straight back. I gazed at the transparent sky and felt a little closer to heaven. Romana told me how to sit and what to do with my legs so that the horse would obey me. Sesil took no notice, of course. He kept stopping and munching tufts of dry grass.

'Your legs are weak but with a bit of practice you'll get him to obey you,' Romana explained.

I was on cloud nine. I knew I had found someone who would be just as important for me as Granny. I fell under Romana's spell. She told me what the plaster on her chin was about. Her dad had given her a thrashing the day before. She told me about nasty kids teasing her because of her limp. And about her love for Sesil. We went on talking for a very long time. So long, in fact, that I forgot I was about to run away from home. I didn't come to my senses until we said goodbye at the bus stop. Two policemen came up to me, holding a photo. Sounding very serious, they said my name and asked if it was me. I nodded. Romana gave me an admiring look and wished me luck. The men in uniform bundled me into their car and drove me home.

'Do you know what time it is?' Mum asked me after she thanked the cops. Her eyes were red from crying. 'Were you trying to punish me, Karolína?' she asked reproachfully. But I was on the top of the world. I didn't regret a thing. After an hour of interrogation we agreed a truce. I would be allowed to go to the riding centre and she would stop bringing the bearded guy home.

But that was rubbish, of course. Totally unrealistic. Women have pussies and men are crazy about them. And on top of that, Mum had the randy Indian princess inside her... She sent the bearded guy packing but soon shacked up with someone new. So I decided to ignore her boyfriends. Whenever she had male visitors I made myself invisible. I would walk around as silently as a ghost not responding to any questions. And I'd quickly get out of the house and head for the riding centre. Later I would go there straight from class, as soon as I'd forced the insipid school lunch down my throat.

Romana's home life was hell. Her dad beat her all the time. What he had wanted was a football player. And then his wife went and gave birth to a girl, and to cap it all, she had one leg shorter than the other. He got plastered on a regular basis and then turned into a devil. Romana prayed every day that he would kick the bucket. We used to meet at the bus stop by a food stall with a badly-drawn picture of a huge hot dog. Romana said it reminded her of a horse's penis. I said I wouldn't know as the only penis I'd seen was the bearded guy's purple sausage. The dilapidated 122 bus stop seemed to us a thing of beauty. We found it easier to breathe there. We could leave everything bad, nasty and annoying behind. We felt liberated at our bus stop. We'd stand there holding hands, shouting and laughing at the tops of our voices. With our polyester trousers loosened, our keys dangling around our necks and stale bread in our school bags. For our horse.

Yes, Sesil was ours. He was an old, fat, Hutzul-Arab grey. Romana had read up on everything. What to feed a horse like this, how to properly clean it with a curry comb and dandy brush. She showed me how to lift Sesil's legs and remove mud and small stones from his hooves with a hoof-pick. Sesil would let us do as we pleased, provided he got something in return. A leftover apple, a piece of mouldy bread or a shrivelled carrot. We rode him every day. Romana even got him to canter. He managed only half a lap but it was her first real riding success. I was still learning how to leap onto Sesil's back. My scrawny muscles were holding me back. And even once I managed to grip his round belly with my legs, I would flop down onto the ground again.

Romana never laughed at me. She insisted that I was getting better and would crack it eventually. And she was right. The horse's movements spurred my body to grow stronger. My movements were no longer uncoordinated and I got fitter and fitter. Suddenly I was able to jump over a vaulting buck at PE, making my teacher's jaw drop. My backbone straightened, my abs tightened. My shoulder blades no longer jutted out. Budding nipples appeared under my white vest. They were sore to the touch. My face lengthened and began to lose its chubby baby shape. Adolescence beckoned. I examined my developing body and observed the way it was changing.

Romana and I spent ages sitting in a hayloft, full of fragrant hay, eating raw sugarbeet we'd nicked from the stables and watching house martins catch fat bluebottles in flight. The sun baked down on the roof tiles. It was melting the tarmac in the yard where a rider was hosing down a horse. The gelding stood there patiently. Sparkling in the sun, the water formed tiny mirrors of liquid on its back.

'There's a peasant in a wide-brimmed straw hat inside him,' I blurted out. Romana raised her eyebrows in incomprehension.

'If I look at people in a special way I can see someone else inside them,' I explained.

'So what does my soul look like?'

I lowered my eyelids and rolled my eyes to the back of my head. 'I see a warrior holding a spear inside you.'

Romana chuckled. 'And what about my legs, are they both the same size?'

I assured her that her soul was fitted out with the most perfect pair of legs I'd ever seen.

Romana turned serious. 'And what's inside my father?'

The peasant turned off the hose, and started scraping the water off the horse's coat with a length of twine.

'I'd have to see him… but maybe there's nothing inside him. Or just a thing… or an animal. It's different with everyone.' I told her about the randy Indian princess inside Mum.

'And what about you?'

Her question took me by surprise. I studied my hands, feet, knees and shoulders for a while. I turned around to get the best possible angle. But I couldn't see anything. 'I can't see into myself, only into other people. God knows who's inside me!' I said and took a big bite out of a beet.

Romana sat for a while extracting a bogey from her nose. When she finally got it out she said she would try to look inside me if I taught her my eye trick. We had a long conversation about invisible creatures. I told her about Granny and showed her the knife she'd given me. Romana liked it. She liked it so much she taught me how to throw it quite well.

The women riders put up with us. The men ignored us. We were just cheeky kids who got under their feet, annoying the grown-ups. All we were good for was sweeping the stables or mucking out. Sometimes, when a rider was in a good mood, he would let us brush down his horse. We would often hang around the showjumping track watching the riders practice. In our heads we jumped the obstacles and spurred the horses. We were happy when one of the women riders let us hand walk her gorgeous palomino mare after practice. The mare's mane floated in the air like silken golden hair. Her name was Isabela and she was a brilliant showjumper. The rider adored her. Isabela was a future champion, certain to bring the riding school money and fame one day. As we held the mare's reins, Romana and I felt as if we had treasure in our hands. Isabela watched us with her beautiful shiny eyes. From time to time she snorted gently. Her sweaty muscular body smelled wonderful. We walked next to her with bated breath. The mare was on heat but we didn't really know what that meant. But Isabela knew only too well. Slowly but resolutely she dragged us towards the paddock where a brown stallion was grazing. Before we could grasp what was going on, Isabela turned around and stuck her hindquarters into a gap between wooden slats. The stallion started trembling. He gave a mighty neigh and jumped up. A long pink pipe shot out of his groin. It gave Isabela's rump a few smacks before digging into her vagina. The mare stood rooted to the spot. She wouldn't let us pull her away.

The rider came dashing out of the changing room, groaning louder than the stallion. We didn't know what to do. Neither did the rider. She ran around shouting 'Oh my God, what have I done to deserve this?'

We just stood there like two useless little dumplings, gaping at the horses mating. The brown stallion's hind legs stamped the ground a few times. Then he climbed off Isabela's back and went back to graze. As if nothing had happened. The mare also pretended nothing had happened. We were frightened and the rider was furious. She called us stupid little sluts. After that she had it in for us. But it didn't make any difference. Eleven months later Isabela gave birth to a velvety little foal.

I met him at the bottle deposit section of our local grocer's. The cashier refused to take the bottle he brought. This type wasn't manufactured in this country, she claimed. He tried to point out that even if it wasn't produced here, it was still made of glass. Therefore she should be a good socialist and oblige her comrade customer. Arms akimbo, the shop assistant started to yell. She'd give him a fucking whacking that would make him spit his teeth out.

In an innocent little voice I asked what the word 'fucking' meant.

The boy gently stroked my hair and explained calmly. 'What it means is that comrade shop assistant is cross, vulgar and illiterate. If she was more articulate she would say she was about to assault me physically.'

The shop assistant went berserk. She grabbed the bottle from his hands, flung it into a bottle crate and tossed the money onto the counter. 'Get the hell out of here!' she screamed. She slammed the door shut.

The boy gave me a wink and vanished somewhere among the

supermarket shelves. I headed for the confectionery. The fancy chocolates were kept on the top shelf. Bags of Milan Assortment, the yummiest chocolate pralines I knew, perched right on top like the queen of sweets. 'Eat me,' they said. I counted out the money, which was burning in my hands. I pursed my lips in disappointment.

'How much are you short?' asked a voice behind my back. Someone gave one of my ears a gentle flick.

'Thirty hellers.' I said.

'Leave it to me,' whispered the boy from the bottle deposit. He put the chocolates in his basket and headed for the till. I followed him. He seemed so grown-up. If you're twelve someone four years older seems almost like an adult. The cashier was taking her time ringing up the items in the shopping baskets. Judging by her vacant eyes and dull expression her break was long overdue. A break from the customers, her manager, small change and burst bags of milk. The boy took the chocolates out of his basket and casually launched into a spiel: 'Comrade! I'm not quite eighteen yet, but my irresponsible mother sent me here to buy cigarettes and some chocolates for my little sister. I wonder if you'd be so kind as to sell me some hardpack Sparta cigarettes.'

The cashier squinted, recovering from her blackout.

The boy flashed her a lovely smile. He got his money out. 'And keep the fifty hellers change,' he said with a conspiratorial smile.

The cashier rang up the Milan Assortment, took the money and handed him the cigarettes. The boy thanked her. On the other side of the cash desk he opened the chocolates. He took one out and slowly placed it in my mouth. Then he stashed the cigarettes in the pocket of his fancy denim jacket. He made sure he said goodbye to everyone. We headed for the exit. Once outside he lit up, taking two long drags.

I savoured the chocolate as it melted in my mouth exposing a crunchy almond. 'Not bad,' I acknowledged his performance. 'And thanks for the Milan... Want one?' The boy shook his head. I noticed red pimples on his cheeks. His Elvis quiff badly needed a wash. 'Arpi,' he introduced himself and offered me a cigarette with a gentlemanly gesture.

'No, that would kill me,' I said, turning down his offer.

Arpi drew on his cigarette, took my hand and said 'Come on, let me show you something.'

We went round the back of the supermarket and stopped in front of a bare concrete wall.

A worn metal staircase attached to the wall seemed to lead right up to heaven. Arpi was already climbing the ladder. I followed him. We reached the tin roof. A grey concrete yard was spread out beneath us. We sat down on a semi-derelict chimney. The yard below was teeming with women in white lab coats. They were holding small banners with portraits of Gottwald and Husák. The faces of the communist party leaders glued to wooden sticks looked like puppets in some bizarre theatre. The file of women marched up and down impassively, shouting slogans.

A bald chap stood on a chair facing the women. He was yelling and flailing his arms about furiously. He kept repeating frantically: 'Comrades! Show me some life, you deadbeats!'

Arpi grinned at me. He said the earlier I got started the better. He wished someone had shoved the first ciggie in his mouth the moment he was born. 'Those living corpses!' he barked, pointing with his chin at the women mindlessly practising the march. I didn't really get what he was talking about but was overcome by a sense of helplessness. The sun caressed my scratched knees. The chocolates were melting in their bag.

The marching rehearsal wasn't going well. The women tottered about the yard, chanting the slogans with a distinct lack of enthusiasm. The man climbed off the chair and smashed it on the floor in a frenzy. I thought he was going to explode and his innards would soil the whole city, dirty though it was already. The white lab coats came to a halt, trying to calm him down, but without success. The man wiped his forehead with a handkerchief. He was breathing heavily. A woman came out of the building and poured some liquid into a glass from the bottle Arpi had just returned. The man downed it in one go. He examined the bottle with interest and, in a voice that sounded calmer now, he asked the women to concentrate. The women in lab coats formed a line.

Arpi produced the box of cigarettes again. I took one without a word and determinedly lit my first cigarette. The sting of the smoke took my breath away. My eyes almost burst out of their sockets. I was desperately panting for fresh air. Arpi roared with laughter. He explained that smoking was an art that had to be acquired. Then the lab coats were given a break and we climbed back down. Arpi courteously invited me to a deserted garage.

Finally here was someone who didn't treat me like a stupid little kid. Arpi radiated calm and had a nice voice. The garage was plastered with posters of bands I had never heard of. The one I liked best showed people with painted faces. One of them looked like a cat. He was leaning on the letter 'I' in a word that spelled KISS. 'I know that word, it's in Hungarian, isn't it? It means… small,' I said, trying to show off.

Arpi thought that was hilarious. He told me it was the name of an English band. He said that during their gigs they often spat blood and belched out smoke. I sat down on a tattered sofa. Arpi offered me another cigarette and turned on his tape-recorder. Some amazing music began to fill the air. It grabbed me by the throat and compressed my diaphragm. I forgot to breathe. Astonished, I asked: 'Who's that?'

Arpi gave me a serious look and announced reverentially that this was Pink Floyd, the twentieth century's most brilliant band. This was the recording of a gig. *Live at Pompeii.*

I tried to inhale without coughing.

'Close your eyes… listen, and inhale gently,' Arpi ordered.

I felt my body absorbing the smoke along with the music as my lungs expanded with great, yet delicate force. I let the smoke course through my lungs for a while. Then I closed my mouth and let it out through my nose. I was intoxicated. My head was spinning. I glanced at Arpi through tears. 'I want to listen to this kind of music as well. Where can I get it?' I whimpered.

He gave a sarcastic laugh. Only *vekslåks,* illegal money-changers, peddled this kind of stuff, he explained. 'But I can give you a tape if you like. If you let me have a pair of your knickers.'

I was taken aback. 'What for? They won't fit you!'

Arpi said he just wanted to fool around with them. But only if the knickers had been worn for at least a day! That was the only way he liked it. His face turned pink. Inside him I could now see the shaved head of an Egyptian priest similar to the one I had seen in a book about the Pyramids. An alluring smile played on the priest's lips. His eyes, traced with thick black eyeliner, reminded me of a serpent. Arpi's face turned serious.

'So what do you say? I'll go out, you take your knickers off and that's it. I won't look. Cross my heart!'

I remembered I had my knife on me, in case anything went wrong. I agreed. Arpi crawled into a wardrobe. I took my knickers off in a flash. I noticed that the yellow lace on the edges was beginning to fray. Arpi came out. He took my knickers and stared at them like treasure trove. Then he stuffed them in his pocket. He gave me a tape and a few cigarettes. And that's how I got to know Pink Floyd and took up smoking.

I remember that moment as if it were yesterday. I was standing by the stable gates. The stable was suffused with sunlight. Flies chased one another playfully around a piece of flypaper. Rays of sun transformed their wings into semiprecious stones. Horses dozed in the afternoon heat, mechanically fanning their bellies with their tails. A velvety dust settled on their skin turning it into pure gold. Leila, July, Pearl and Lombard stood to the left, Hakim, Ambal, Yaga and Sesil to the right. I remember the personality of each and every one of them. I can recall exactly what made each of them buck and what might scare them. There was nothing that gave me more pleasure than to press my lips against their soft muzzles.

The sensation I enjoyed most of all was lying down on Sesil's back. I would close my eyes and listen to his breathing. I could hear the rumbling of his bowels and his powerful heartbeat. Sometimes he would move, which made his joints crackle. He would give a loud snort. Eyes half closed, legs dangling, I was without a worry in the world. I lay on his back like a rag doll, just chilling out. Sesil was very gentle. As he slowly turned to walk into his box, he would gingerly shift his weight from one foot to another. I felt completely secure again. Like in my mother's womb.

I spent hours gazing into Sesil's sad, obsidian-coloured eyes. He was a pensioner. Sometimes they made him pull a cart laden with straw or, after the races, carry children. His career as a vaulting horse was long over. Riders exploited his serene nature to calm down young, nervous fillies. Whenever a horse was frightened, Sesil would be sent for. He was also used to help load horses onto the trailer. Young horses would buck until they saw Sesil. Unperturbed, he would slowly clamber up the ramp, grunt and start feeding.

Romana and I used to groom him every day, scraping him clean and weaving daisies into his mane. I borrowed a book on farm animals from the library. We would hold Sesil's head for hours on end and memorise: forehead, poll, muzzle. We would run our fingers along his smooth coat: withers, croup, hock, fetlock. We tried to commit every ripple of his graceful body to memory. We tried to guess where his spleen, heart and windpipe might be. We learned where his temporal bone and mandible were located. We rattled off in a whisper: 'Os temporale, os nasale, mandibula, musculus semispinalis capitis.' It sounded like an incantation. Sesil squinted sleepily and let us scratch between his ears. We spent most of our time at the riding centre. We pretended to the school nurse that we were down with a cold. We skived off Young Pioneer meetings and sneaked away from the Labour Day parade. We managed to get ourselves kicked out of the Spartakiad team because of our dismal performance. We were hard to track down, like the tiny grey birds that used to peck oats from the feeders.

The summer holidays were about to begin. Instead of classes we all just mooched about at school. The teachers were deciding our end of year grades. School desks were being sanded down. The time had come for our first girls' outing. By now I had became expert at lying to Mum. Without batting an eyelid. Arpi concocted a beautifully-phrased teacher's note informing parents of a forthcoming two-day school trip, complete with a perfectly-forged teacher's signature. Mum never even dreamed anything was amiss. She was happy to have the flat to herself for one of her sex romps. She bought me some tinned meat, bread and sweets. She filled a bottle with a raspberry-flavoured drink made with Vitacit powder. I packed a sleeping bag, thermals and warm socks.

Romana and I arrived at the riding centre in the early afternoon. We holed up in the hayloft, waiting for everyone to leave, for the evening feed to finish and the stables to be locked. The night guard was an old guy, permanently drunk. As soon as everyone left he disappeared into his cabin and opened a bottle of vodka. The sun sank languidly below the horizon, turning the sky bright orange. Young swallows played tag. We lay on the unmowed lawn next to the paddock, eating salty luncheon meat and watching the pink clouds slowly drift by. I lit up. The hot wind blew its promise of love into my hair. I passed the cigarette to Romana. She was beaming with joy. She dragged on the cigarette cautiously. She peeled scabs off her legs and fed them to the ants. A horse neighed. Its high-pitched voice silenced a thrush sitting high up in a pine tree. Silence fell. Only the wind gently brushed the meadow, and field poppies, reminiscent of wolf cubs' bloodied eyes, frolicked in the grass.

I dreamed I was a swallow, flying low above a river. Its brightness dazzled me. I felt its warmth on my tummy. The river was a stream of lava glowing gold. I was flying fast. Straight ahead at first, then abruptly changing direction and shooting upwards vertiginously. Right into the blazing sun. It blinded me. I felt ecstatic. A wave of euphoria swept my body. I woke up screaming.

A couple of days later Matilda appeared at Sesil's box. Her piercing blue eyes drilled into me with a force that took my breath away. She tucked her blonde hair behind her ears and smiled in a peculiar way, as if reluctant to reveal her teeth. 'Not practising today?' she asked, patting the horse's neck.

She was tall. In her skintight jodhpurs and figure-hugging T-shirt, we couldn't fail to notice how beautiful she was. Romana and I exchanged glances but remained stubbornly silent.

'I'm Matilda,' she said and extended her hand.

Grown-ups shaking our hands was certainly not something we were used to. Suspiciously we glanced at her hand and at each other and back at her hand.

Matilda laughed. 'I've been watching you for a while now and I think you're rather clever kids!'

Eventually Romana took her hand.

'You're Karolína, aren't you,' Matilda asked me and all I could do was nod dumbly. I found her fragrance intoxicating. Cinnamon mixed with fruit of some sort. My eyes rolled back in my head. Hidden inside her I saw a queen. A queen standing proud. An exquisitely ornamented tiara made her searching emerald eyes shine. They seemed to look right into my heart.

'We're not practising today, Sesil's paddock has been overrun by wild colts,' said Romana as she gently pinched my bum. 'And as you well know, we're not allowed to ride, we have to do it secretly in the paddock!'

I came to my senses.

Matilda slowly put her arms akimbo. 'So how about I get comrade director to let you use the arena... and, by the way, skip the formalities, call me Matilda.'

Romana and I burst out laughing. Yeah, very funny. Sure, the director will let us use the arena. Comrade director enjoyed god-like status. Communist style, that is. People spoke of him with fear. Of his power. Nobody dared to make a move without his approval. He kept tabs on everything that went on. And anyone who defied him got the sack. He lorded it over the horses' lives and the riders' triumphs. He was a greedy son-of-a-bitch. With his safe seat on the Regional Council, he ruled the riding centre with an iron fist. Rumour had it he had a TV set and a leather sofa in his office. He rode the wildest stud. And the stallion obeyed him at the slightest touch of the reins. It trotted like a meek little lamb. The same horse that wouldn't hesitate to kick the brains out of our heads. The director straddled it proudly, like a general. Men of his kind are oblivious of kids. To him we were nothing but vermin.

The queen's eyes blazed, turning the deepest marshy green. We fell silent.

Matilda turned on her heel and marched right up to the director's office. 'Just you wait!' she shouted, her clear voice darting around the stables like a fly.

Two hours later we were standing in the huge riding arena. Sesil wore a strange harness. Matilda led him on a white lunge rein. 'This is a surcingle, girls' she said, pointing her whip at the leather handles protruding from Sesil's back. 'Try it out at a walk first!' Romana hobbled up to Sesil, tentatively grabbing the handles. For a while she limped awkwardly alongside Sesil. Then with a stamp of her feet she jumped onto the horse's back. Light as a feather.

Matilda told her how to exercise. How to sit astride and where her centre of gravity should be. 'Excellent! Now try it at a canter,' she shouted and clicked her tongue at Sesil. The horse shot into the ring like a guided missile. His mane turned into white ribbons blowing in the wind. His nostrils flared. His eyes glistened. He snorted gently along with the rhythm of the canter. He looked ten years younger. Romana crossed and recrossed her legs, then did the first part of a flank. It was as if she were performing some weird dance. Her shorter leg lengthened miraculously and she was suddenly transformed into a normal, vivacious girl.

I decided to have a go, too. The handles were really useful. Matilda explained in plain language how to vault on. It's a simple little trick. I had to run alongside Sesil for a while, matching the rhythm of his canter. Holding tight to the surcingle handles, I planted my stiffened legs sharp on the ground and swung myself up. Shooting high above the horse's back, I spread my legs gracefully in the air and touched down gently. It felt different. An even canter. Suddenly I was able to focus on my body. My lower back relaxed. My spine vibrated in time with the canter. I straightened up, holding my head high.

'Now, slowly raise your arms,' came Matilda's instructions. I felt as if I were flying. I plucked up the courage to kneel on Sesil's back and… stood up. I stood on the horse for about three seconds. But to me it felt as if I were up in the sky watching the world down below, as if I were about to jump out of my skin before returning into my awkward body. Then I fell off.

We were learning. Matilda explained the difference between compulsory and freestyle exercises. She showed us the technique for mastering ground jumps. Practising every day, we were so exhausted we kept falling asleep on the bus on our way home. Mum hardly recognised me. Her wilful, weedy little girl was growing into a confident sportswoman. I couldn't give a damn about her boyfriends. I only went home to eat, sleep and shower. I became adept at copying other people's work at school and scraped through with Bs, one C at the most. Once I even managed to get As and just two Bs. That was the time my Mum shacked up with one of those shady *vekslåks*. He gave her vouchers for Tuzex, the foreign currency shop. She bought me a Walkman. A blue Walkman with orange headphones. That day the first summer storm thundered over our housing estate. As soon as the rain stopped I went out, a cassette from Arpi in my Walkman. I found myself transported into another world. I thought I could hear some steps behind me and turned around to check if there was someone following me. The noise of a throbbing machine mingled with laughter. An insane human scream nearly shattered my eardrums, and a guitar solo carried me into another dimension. I walked around the estate. The rain had turned it into a mirror. Puddles stared blindly into the sky refracting sunrays back into the universe. As if broadcasting desperate messages from our socialist world. I suddenly saw everything in a new light. Even the grimy building sites had something going for them. I quickened my pace propelled by the pounding beat. As the second track started I noticed a huge lorry dumping tons of sand. Dust floated in the air. It reminded me of a sandstorm our geography teacher had told us about. Tipped upwards, the body of the lorry looked like a prehistoric bird's open beak. Sand slid into a hole. Builders reclining on their shovels smoked roll-ups while I was high on Pink Floyd.

It really rocked. It was like nothing I'd ever known before. Listening to *The Dark Side of the Moon* on horseback induced in me the same state as the joint Arpi had once offered. As the horse cantered the music reverberated through my body. I was both medium and message, receiving and transmitting at the same time. Sesil caught the vibe. He plugged into the drumbeat, galloping as if he could hear it. I felt I was absolute perfection. My muscles worked effortlessly. Methodically. Without the slightest impediment. My body was transformed into a machine that ran all by itself. I stopped thinking. I felt the horse's warm body moving between my legs. I was becoming more and more aware of the pleasure generated by the movement. My hairless pussy rubbed against Sesil's hide. It kept growing. Swelling. It was getting bigger and moister. It went all gooey and hot. It kept expanding. It engulfed Sesil and the riding centre. A million hot tongues licked my clitoris. Pleasure slowed down my movements. I sank my pelvis into Sesil's back. Deeper and deeper. I felt a tremendous shudder inside my pussy. A spasm passed through my body. It was out of this world. That's when the song finished. Sesil came to a halt. I heard joyous clapping.

Matilda stood in the middle of the vaulting arena, shouting: 'Bravo! Karolína, what you did just now wasn't simply exercising, it was dancing! That's just what I want!'

I felt hugely embarrassed. I was completely unnerved by the pleasure I'd just felt. My own body had given me a scare. It felt mysterious and out of control. I wondered if I'd fallen ill. My breasts felt tender. Muddled thoughts whirled around my head. I stood breathlessly by Sesil's side. A sly smile on Matilda's face made me wonder if she'd noticed anything. She patted me on the back. 'We must have music to exercise by,' I exhaled. The queen inside her nodded her approval. She smiled. Her teeth glittered like polished red apples.

A week later a tape recorder with speakers appeared in the riding hall. Matilda wanted to show us off in a demonstration performance at the next championship. She hoped that it would convince the director to let her start a vaulting team. Compulsory exercises. Freestyle exercises. Everything had to run as smoothly as clockwork. Exactly in line with the horse's canter. So Romana and I started slogging away. We would train every day. We learned how to do the flag, the scales, how to swing off to the outside from seat astride and kneel with arms raised. My greatest problem was with the static exercises where I had to keep in position without moving while Sesil cut away. I couldn't keep my balance for very long. I kept falling off, hitting my pelvis on the hard handles. My hips were often covered in bruises. Romana was best at cartwheels and pirouettes. She could turn deftly around her own axis without losing her balance or the rhythm of the horse's canter. One day I hurt myself really badly as I crossed my arms in an unfortunate way. The move threw me off Sesil's saddle. I fell on my back like a log and got winded. I gasped for air like a fish out of water. For a brief moment I relived the horror of drowning. But Matilda knew no mercy. She helped me back onto my feet. And as soon as I was able to breathe even a little, she forced me to clamber back onto Sesil. I had to exercise until I forgot about my fear.

She knew what she was doing. Each day she pushed our limits a little bit further. Quite soon I was experimenting with even the hardest hanging exercises. Before I knew it I was hanging off the horse, head down, my foot through the surcingle loop. Sesil was cantering. The fingers of my outstretched arms brushed the ground and I could feel my lunch in my throat. After four strides at a canter I was sick. Romana and Matilda guffawed watching me wipe the undigested noodles off my face.

'You mustn't eat for at least three hours before practice,' Matilda explained.

I gave up lunches. I would suck on some sugar cubes to keep going. I was as thin as a stick insect. After practice we had to wipe Sesil's rump. We would rub him down with straw until he was completely dry. We would pat his fat tummy and woo him with the most ardent declarations of love. In the evenings I would catch the last bus home. I'd find Mum snoring away in front of the TV, still on. Matilda later showed us pair exercises. I was the first to vault on. Holding the grip with my left hand, I reached my right hand out to Romana. She ran alongside Sesil matching her stride to his canter. Then she bounced hard on both feet and vaulted on, swinging one leg over. She tugged at me so hard she made me slide off the horse. We both tumbled into the sand. It took us nearly a week to learn how to vault on as a pair. Eventually Romana and I became perfectly attuned. In the basic seat, with my arms out to the sides, I could feel her budding breasts gently pushing against my back. Sesil cantered to the music from the speakers. Romana's breath caressed the crown of my head. When we performed a flag with her sitting on my shoulders, her perspiring thighs rubbed against my neck. We swung gracefully from one side of the horse to the other. Romana even managed a splendid headstand as I held on to her waist. We passed seamlessly from one move to the next. We were transformed into dancing Siamese twins, merging into a single living sculpture with the grey horse. Matilda was very pleased with us. She sewed us short red skirts. In our white T-shirts and white trainers we looked like cute little fly agaric mushrooms. Red-and-white Siamese twins with tiny peas for breasts. Adorable.

It was shaping up to be the most wonderful Saturday in my life. The smell of *bundáskenyér*, the French toast, Hungarian style, wafting from the frying pan drew me out of bed. Mum was standing over the stove, her robe loosely tied. Strong coffee spewed from the percolator's innards. Strong enough to wake a corpse. I sat down at the kitchen table. Did I like it, did I need more ketchup, was it salty enough, Mum kept asking. She fussed about me as if I were a little princess. Her sudden solicitude started to worry me.

'You need a proper meal! You clever girl, you!' she cooed and even offered me a ciggie.

At first I pretended I didn't want one.

Mum grinned: 'What do you take me for? I've known for ages that you smoke!'

We sat on our mini balcony drinking coffee. Blue smoke rings rose from our mouths and dissolved in the air. I noticed the first grey hairs starting to invade Mum's black mane. We sat watching the white line an airplane scribbled into the sky and listened to the zebra finches tweeting in our next door neighbour's cage. I realised how nice it felt being with Mum. For a moment I had a childish urge to cuddle up to her breasts.

'Who would have thought that my two-left-feet of a girl would ever get this far,' she said, laughing, and went off to pick up the phone that started ringing in the hall.

I stubbed my ciggie out and went to whiten my trainers. I wanted everything to be just perfect on my big day. In my mind I ran through the exercises I would do during the demo as I rubbed chalk powder into the dirty canvas.

'*Istenem!*' exclaimed Mum. Surprise mingled with horror in her voice. I pricked up my ears. '*Istenem*, my God!' she kept repeating. The unhappy *Istenem* floating around the hallway made me get up from the floor.

'What's happened?' I asked when she put the receiver down.

She wouldn't answer. She went back to the balcony and lit up again.

It should have been the most wonderful Saturday in my life. If only that phone call hadn't come. If only the boiler at my aunties' house in Miskolc hadn't broken down and if only they hadn't kept their windows shut at night. If, if, if… if pigs could fly. A neighbour found them. Like three enchanted princesses except that their bodies had gone cold. For a while I stood in the hallway, staring at the phone. Waiting for someone to call and say it was just a sick joke. Then I went back to my trainers. I could hardly see what I was doing. My tears dripped onto the canvas, smudging it an ugly grey-brown. Mum was sobbing on the balcony. She said I must try not to think about it. But I couldn't get out of my head the image of the three alabaster-white women with long plaited hair whom I had seen that summer. I couldn't help picturing them in the morgue being dressed and laid into their coffins.

'I hope someone's going to give Márta a shave,' I blurted out on our way to the riding centre.

Mum stifled her laughter with a handkerchief. She had downed two shots of apricot *pálinka* and found everything amusing. A warm wind was blowing, playfully knocking juicy mulberries off the trees. The fruit dropped into the drinks of the people hanging around the shabby street kiosk drinking beer. The neighing of excited horses filled the riding centre. A woman's voice announced the results of the Captain Jan Nálepka Memorial Race. The winner was comrade director, riding Zadiel. Romana and I warmed up and got changed. Matilda spat on us three times for good luck before we made our grand entrance into the sand-strewn arena. Sesil's coat sparkled in the sun. With a dignified air he placed his oiled hooves on the newly-mown lawn. Matilda was wearing a red riding outfit and leather boots. She had bought a new whip with a tiny multicoloured pompom. Spectators had already taken their seats in the modest stands. Mum sat in the first row. I could smell mustard and boiled sausages. Someone shouted Romana's name. The woman's voice on the loudspeaker drily announced the final number. The brass band on the airwaves fell silent and the third track on Arpi's tape reverberated through the air. Pink Floyd knocked the spectators sideways. The stands fell silent. Matilda clicked her tongue at Sesil and swished her whip, just for the fun of it. The multicoloured pompom at the end of the whip flew up like a tiny hummingbird.

I leapt onto Sesil's back. My little scarlet skirt swayed to the stride of his canter. Sesil latched on to the drumbeat at once. My brain transmitted the image of the first exercise to my body. My muscles obediently followed my thoughts. My spine vibrated and relaxed. I didn't even have to try very hard. The hours of practice ensured my moves were on autopilot. I was aware only of the music. It was no effort at all. My heart pumped oxygenated blood into every single cell of my body. The percussion catapulted me into another world. The stands decked out in little banners vanished. I found myself in a circus ring. I was wearing a glittery black dress. It caressed my thighs, as light as gossamer. The horse cantered and its golden-red harness sparkled with fiery lights. The audience applauded. A man threw his top hat in the air. Kids were chewing on their nougat bars and posh ladies in lace gowns fanned themselves. The music carried me onto the horse's back. I inhaled the intoxicating smell of oil lamps. I performed one trick after another. Each one more beautiful and dangerous than the last. I didn't recognise myself. I was different. All grown up. I grew muscular arms, long legs and firm, full breasts. I couldn't stop admiring myself. That was when it clicked and I realised who was hidden inside me. I stood on the cantering horse and vaulted off hard. I sliced through the canvas of the big top like a razor blade. The sun glued my eyes together, blinding me for a moment. I stretched out my arms and started coming down. Very slowly. It lasted a long time. I was transformed into a circus artist, an equestrienne. I lived several lives in the brief instant before my feet touched the ground. The music stopped. I landed on the hard surface like an accomplished performer. The equestrienne bowed. The audience applauded. So did Mum. She had put down her beer and stood by the stand. Her eyes had lost their unearthly lustre. The horny Indian princess was gone and the person waving to me was an ordinary, happy mum.

Success was sweet. The memory of my dead aunties was banished completely. Everyone was smiling at me. People showered us with compliments. We were treated to corn on the cob and soft drinks. Matilda elegantly fielded the questions addressed to us: 'Who sewed these charming little red skirts? What do you call this sport?' Sesil strode proudly back to the stables and greedily stuck his noble head into a bucket of sweet molasses. We chatted while we rubbed his belly down with straw. Matilda was cleaning the surcingle and a mysterious smile played about her lips. When the happy hum of well-fed horses had drowned out the last spectator's voice, a huge shadow appeared behind us.

Comrade director in person had condescended to honour us, miserable worms, with his presence. He looked us over sternly, making me feel like a piece of paper pinned to the wall. 'You may practise and compete,' he barked. 'On one condition! You have to scrap that awful imperialist music immediately and find something ideologically acceptable!' He turned on his heel and marched off briskly.

'What does ideologically acceptable mean?' Romana asked.

Matilda cast a disdainful glance after the director and offered a dry explanation: 'Something that won't upset the comrades!'

A June downpour drummed monotonously on the corrugated roof of the hayloft. We were sitting by the open stable gate watching huge bubbles of rain collecting in a puddle. The rumble of thunder frightened Leila, a young mare in the box next to Sesil's. She neighed restlessly, kicking the stable door every now and then. The rain smelled of acacia blossom. Suddenly I felt an irresistible urge to stick my hand under the leaky drainpipe. Then I remembered that the roof had been given a coat of lead paint last week. I quickly wiped my hand on my tracksuit and took a piece of sugar beet from Romana.

'We'll start a girls' vaulting team,' Matilda had announced. 'We'll bring in more girls and enter competitions!'

Romana said she couldn't wait to get away from home. 'We'll get to travel up and down the country, maybe even abroad,' she mused. There was another clap of thunder.

Matilda ruffled our hair affectionately. She praised us for being clever and talented girls and said the whole world would soon be at our feet. If we practised hard, we could achieve great things. Her words worked like magic. I felt like I had grown a mighty eagle's wings. Her words made me feel strong, I became more confident and articulate.

The political drivel at school no longer got me down. Our history teacher waxed lyrical about the Košice Government Declaration of 1945.

I retorted icily: 'But it was just daylight robbery! My granny was no traitor, yet they took her tavern away and evicted her and grandpa. They had to move all the way to Cheb, right at the other end of the country!'

The teacher narrowed her eyes and whispered in horror: 'Keep your voice down, my dear, you never know who's listening!'

But I wouldn't keep my voice down. I wanted to shout from rooftops that I was free and special. Unstoppable. I recruited four other girls for our vaulting team. They lived in the high-rise blocks opposite ours. They used to get so bored that they would spend their time setting fire to their neighbours' postboxes. They weren't afraid of horses and picked up all the tricks with incredible speed. It took them only two weeks to master the sideways mount and ground jump. They fluttered on top of Cecil's back as light as butterflies. I half-closed my eyes and inside their sinewy bodies saw acrobats on a trapeze.

'We'll make it to the world championship,' Romana whispered frenziedly. 'We'll be famous. And my mum will be allocated a company flat. You know what that means? She'll be able to leave dad!' This was her mantra. She kept repeating it whenever she no longer had the strength to mount the horse after two hours' practice. The thought helped her get through the most difficult exercises.

Comrade director gave us our own changing rooms. They had lockers covered in horse stickers, a few chairs and a rickety table. A veritable kingdom. I still see it before my eyes. There were bits of stale bread hidden on the shelves and dirty socks drying on the radiator. The windows had worn tracksuits hanging on them instead of curtains. The all-pervading smell was of manure mingling with the strong fragrance of hoof ointment.

Matilda was a hard taskmaster. We polished our routines in daily training sessions. We pointed our toes so hard it gave us foot cramps. Matilda devised specially-tailored exercises for us. We now practised to Tchaikovsky, who was ideologically more acceptable. The trick riders' tanned legs flashed to the rhythm of piano preludes, creating the illusion of carefree summer holidays in the Russian countryside. That, at least, was the image conjured up by the set books in our Russian classes. 'You've got to visualise your routines! You have to get them into your bloodstream!' Matilda explained.

We had to absorb the exercises, make them completely automatic and concentrate solely on music during practice. Every night before going to sleep I went through my moves in my head. I would vault on, kneel, spread my arms out in three canter strides and smoothly move into scissors on Sesil's back. Next I did a flag and stand on the horse. I finished my routine with a fast ground jump and a full flank, ending in a vault-off. Everything was timed meticulously. The whole routine took no more than three minutes. Even the slightest hesitation would make me miss a canter stride and lose time.

The last night before the championships I dropped by Arpi's. He had managed to get hold of a real electric guitar and an amplifier and played me a song he'd written. It was a song about the sun, peace and love. His long fingers leapt up and down the strings like the legs of a spider spinning a cobweb. He had a good voice, if a bit hoarse. I rewarded him with a new pair of knickers, worn for a week. He gave me a pack of cigarettes and a new Emgeton cassette tape. A surprise for me, he said.

The following day I got up at 4 a.m. Mum was still fast asleep. I went to the balcony to have my coffee and first ciggie of the day. The sky was an innocent mauve. Somewhere in the street a lorry engine was starting. The overheated prefab blocks of flats radiated warmth as their inhabitants rolled about in their sweat-soaked beds. I put on my Chinese trainers, grabbed my backpack and slammed the door shut behind me. Sleepy men with briefcases were waiting for the bus on their way to the Saturday shift. I put on my headphones and turned on my Walkman. King Crimson, Arpi's latest discovery, nearly blasted my brain out of my skull. My trip on the 94 bus turned into a bizarre video clip. *Schizoid Man* filled the entire bus. The workmen played rummy, slapping the cards on the briefcases on their knees and guffawing away. The smell of their smoked bacon lunch coming from their briefcases mixed with the odour of their unwashed bodies and burning diesel. I will never forget that smell. Two men in muddy clodhoppers dozed off, heads propped against the bus windows. The countryside rolled past, changing slowly. After a while the prefab blocks disappeared from view. The music lifted me off my seat. I was floating somewhere alongside the moving Ikarus bus. I felt euphoric. Thoughts of what lay ahead flitted through my mind. I grinned at my own reflection in the window like a small child.

I was the first of the team to arrive at the riding centre. Matilda was already there, trying to rouse the drunken night guard and telling him to unlock the stables. She was wearing a T-shirt with a big red tongue sticking out and I decided I would beg Arpi to drum up a Rolling Stones tape for her. I groomed Cecil before Romana and the other girls arrived. Their eyes were sparkling and they were agog with excitement. We festooned Sesil with cornflowers. He looked like a bride. Just before seven, our driver tooted his horn in the yard. We loaded up with oats, hay and straw. Romana banged her head on a metal crossbar. Another girl caught her finger in the box where the bridles were kept.

Matilda laughed and shouted at us: 'Get into the trailer, chop-chop, I don't want you to maim yourselves before we even start!'

Sesil whinnied gently. The trailer door slammed shut. The driver, an odd-looking short chap with a toothpick in his mouth started the engine.

The national championship was held at the Agrocomplex, a vast exhibition centre, a classic example of socialist brutalism in architecture. It was used as a venue for showing off pedigree bulls, tractors and all the other achievements of socialist agriculture. We were put up at halls of residence where agriculture students got drunk every night. Cracked washbasins, torn lino and scratched Formica. Beds that were falling apart, no hot water. We were issued food vouchers and spent two hours queuing for sausages in the only cafeteria that was open. We couldn't take our eyes off the muscular Czech junior team. We admired the horses the other vaulting teams performed on. The place was swarming with contestants. There were teams from all over the country, even some from the GDR! The neighing of horses and the brass music blaring from the loudspeakers gave me a headache. We unloaded Sesil and parked him in the stables. Everyone smirked at the fat grey horse who begged passers-by for carrots.

Matilda showed us to the changing rooms and warned us not to do anything silly. 'We can't afford an accident, understood?' she stressed and went to register our names with the judges.

Romana took me by the hand. 'Let's go and check this place out,' she said with a smile.

We elbowed our way through the spectators beginning to fill the stands. Next to the flashing lights of a merry-go-round and shooting gallery we discovered a stall selling the local new wine, *burčiak*.

Romana took a shine to the boy who sold tickets for the chair swing ride. She chatted him up in no time claiming she came from Paris and had her own horse. She said a few words in French, sounding as if she had a clothes peg on her nose. The ploy worked and he gave us a free ride. 'He smells so lovely,' Romana whispered.

A song by the disco star Michal David blasted from the loudspeakers. A few frightened kids squealed on the helter-skelter.

'Let's find our team,' I said wearily.

Romana said goodbye to her chair swing man. He gave her some plastic vampire teeth from the shooting gallery.

Crowds of trick riders had already assembled at the stable door. They were sitting on a low wall and mocked Romana's shorter leg. A mean boy mimicked her walk. With an exaggerated limp, he shouted: 'Hop, jump and limp, you're a loser and a wimp!' It was horrible. I leapt on a crate of oats behind the kids and stared intently at the boy, trying to cast a spell over him. When he looked at me I took out my knife and slowly passed it across my throat. I accompanied the gesture with a frown that was so stern that the boy got the message and stopped. Romana pretended she didn't give a toss. But in the changing rooms she hissed that she would let that moron have it. Stage fright was starting to get the better of us. We rubbed our hands together to keep warm and cracked jokes to cheer each other up.

'Ten minutes and we're on,' Matilda announced. There was tension in her eyes although she tried to disguise it with a smile.

We put the surcingle on Sesil and came out of the stables. We had to wait for the Czech team from Frenštát to finish their compulsories. The judges, seated around the arena, were taking notes with a self-important air. The last rider finished, the team bowed and cantered out of the arena. When our team was announced no applause greeted us from the stands. We were newcomers. We ran into the ring, lined up and bowed in unison. Matilda loosened Sesil's white lunge lead. He launched into a majestic canter.

All of us, except for Romana, left the ring and waited with bated breath. The first bars of Tchaikovsky's Piano Concerto No. 1 in B flat minor rang out around the ring. The judges looked up in surprise. Nobody had performed to music before. I felt as if I was back in our riding hall and this was just a run-of-the-mill practice. Romana performed like a goddess. Her half mill came out absolutely perfect. I'd never seen anyone point their toes like she did. Sesil cantered around snorting happily.

Then it was my turn. I ran alongside the horse for a while getting ready for the mount. I stamped hard on the ground and swiftly leapt onto Cecil's back. The world around me, myself included, ceased to exist. Time came to a standstill. I was an equestrienne. There was just her and her trick riding, her movements in perfect harmony with those of the horse.

We all did brilliantly on that day. None of us made the slightest mistake. We got top marks. Behind the scenes everyone talked about us as the discovery of the season. Performing to music was a big hit. All the other teams envied us Sesil's stately canter. They crowded in to take a look at him. And the chief judge came in person to compliment Romana on her exceptional performance! That night we celebrated our triumph in the first round. Matilda went partying with the other coaches and we stayed on the chair swing until midnight and stuffed our faces with candyfloss. The fairground boy treated us to some *burčiak*. It tasted like grape juice mixed with champagne. I felt my leg muscles relax, and started to laugh for no reason.

Romana's fairground beau tried to kiss me. I shuddered. 'Leave me alone or you'll be sorry!' I yelled.

The boy waved his hand with disdain. 'Daft virgin!'

I lashed out at him with my choicest Hungarian swearwords, calling him a *kibaszott fasz*, fucked-up prick, and went off after Romana. My feet turned into balloons. The multicoloured caravan lights merged into a huge flickering river of red. I drifted along with a crowd of people who had gathered in front of a stage. A magician was making green budgies disappear. Romana must have spent a good two hours whizzing around on the chair swing. The silvery chains jangled and she laughed, kicking her legs high in the air. Until she was sick. A stream of candyfloss and *burčiak* came pouring down on the heads of people standing beneath the ride. Some thought it had started to rain. The fairground boy stopped the ride and sent Romana packing. We decided we might as well go back to our shabby dorm and go to bed.

The next day we drank some gherkin brine for our first hangover. At the cafeteria they were dishing out overcooked *grenadír marš*.

Swollen-eyed as we were, we nevertheless turned in another brilliant performance. When the last trick rider on our team finished her freestyle exercises we got a standing ovation. Everyone knew they were applauding the champions.

We were an overnight sensation. Newspapers wrote about us. Mum cut out a photo of us performing. It was a grainy black-and-white picture and you couldn't make us out in it at all. Mum didn't care. She put it in a wooden frame and proudly displayed it in her bedroom. The world was my very own, shiny oyster. That wonderful feeling of lightheadedness! Competitions and demo performances forged us into a well-oiled team. We were laying the foundations of a new, modern school of equestrian vaulting. We participated in competitions all over Czechoslovakia, once we even got to Hungary. A day before that trip an octopus grew in my belly. Its mighty tentacles squeezed my insides and its suckers stuck to the lining of my womb, expanding and squeezing it over and over again. It felt as if a plunger had latched onto my ovaries. My breasts swelled and cramps kept waking me up all night. In the morning I awoke to a blood-stained day. My bedsheet was all red and my pyjama bottoms were stuck to my pussy. 'I'm bleeding!' I screamed.

Mum rushed out of the bathroom, glanced at the bed and said 'Well, well, well!' and slapped me on the face, which turned red instantly. She smiled in such a weird way that I thought she must have gone round the bend.

'What was that for?' I said putting my hand to my cheek and staring at the red stain. It was the shape of Africa.

'You got your period. Go and take a shower and use a sanitary towel,' she said matter-of-factly and went to the larder to get a packet of them.

'Why did you have to slap me?'

She explained that she had also got a slap across the face from Granny and that one day, when I'd be a mother, I should also slap my daughter's face when she got her first period. 'It's a family tradition. It's to make a girl blush and feel embarrassed... because she's turned into a woman.'

I didn't understand a word. My belly was on fire. I stared at the sanitary pad Mum had thrust in my face. It was a long thick greyish-white object wrapped in netting. *This is what I'm supposed to put on my delicate pussy?* I thought to myself.

Mum made me get up. She recited all the things I wasn't allowed to do while menstruating. It turned out to be quite a list of bans and prohibitions. I wasn't allowed to go swimming, to dance, wear a miniskirt, go on a trampoline, or for a bladder or gynaecological check-up, or wear tight trousers.

'Is there anything left I am allowed to do?'

Mum gave it some thought and said I was allowed to be 'moody' and could now join her in scouring the shops for 'under-the-counter' goods. This was my transition to womanhood. My initiation rite was an hour spent queuing up for sanitary towels. The stiff, unyielding blocks scratched my pussy and made me waddle like a duck. Blood glued my pubic hair to the netting. Sometimes it would get dry and those times, when I changed my pad, I would pull out a few pubic hairs.

I was convinced everyone could see IT. The pad stuck out of my trousers, it got soaked through, it moved around. I found a pair of loose trousers and tied a jumper around my waist. The competition suddenly turned into a nightmare. The thought of having to stuff the huge, shapeless pad into the tight shorts under my skirt tormented me. 'Does my sanitary pad show?' I pestered Romana several times a day. She would take a good look at my bum and whisper conspiratorially: 'Don't worry, it doesn't.' She had not yet had her first period, and was concerned and sympathetic. 'Is it painful?' she asked, stroking my bloated belly.

I felt piercing pain every time the wheels of the horse trailer struck a pothole. The journey to Hungary was torture: the boiling heat, tepid bottled water and filthy toilets at petrol stations. An endless line of cars at the border. The paranoid customs officers took our trailer apart screw by screw. They poked the straw with a long wire to make sure we weren't trying to smuggle something out of the country. We sat on the kerb next to the trailer watching the customs officials confiscate some nylons from the owner of a white Skoda MB. The woman tried to persuade an official that these were gifts for her extended family but he wouldn't fall for it. She was carrying enough nylons to dress every woman in Budapest.

It was early evening when we arrived at the riding hall where the competition was held. We were put up in ramshackle plastic huts close to the stables. The canteen had laminated tablecloths and the toilets wouldn't flush. The portrait of party leader János Kádár was covered in fly shit. A Soviet flag hung limply from a post in the heat, looking like the decomposing cadaver of a dragon. A huge red sun was setting above the endless pancake-flat countryside. The sun seemed to be sinking into the dry earth melting it into caramel. A hot breeze brought the whinneying of horses galloping across the *puszta*, the great Hungarian plain.

The wonderful smell of tomato-and-pepper *lecsó* stew wafted in from the kitchen. In a sing-song voice a cook with a gorgeous tan said, enjoy your meal, kids, '*Jó étvágyat, gyerekek!*'

The shapeless sanitary pad bulged out of my blue shorts. It felt like I had a penis between my legs. I swapped skirts with Romana to be on the safe side since hers was slightly longer. Matilda had been forcing lemons down my throat since early morning. It would reduce the bleeding, she said. But the unbearable heat pumped huge blasts of menstruation blood out of me at regular intervals. I didn't even feel like a cigarette. I was dizzy. 'I think I might bleed to death,' I mumbled.

Matilda managed to procure a bag of ice somewhere. She placed it on my stomach and said, 'Don't be silly! Women are made of tougher stuff!'

It finally dawned on me why this wave of exhaustion swept over Mum regularly every month and why she didn't feel like doing anything around the house on those days. I wished I could go under a general anaesthetic. Just wake me up when it's over! But the competition loomed relentless, and pale and shaky as I was, I had to line up next to Romana. I scurried into the arena with the other girls. I wished I could go to bed instead of performing. The whip cracked and Cecil started trotting majestically. I was the last one on. I stood facing the crowded stand and was aware of blood oozing out of my body. Everyone seemed to be staring between my legs and whispering: 'She's got her period!' But I got going. Sesil's regular canter and the warmth radiating from his back calmed me down. My brain switched to autopilot and summoned up all the moves.

I was in the middle of the full mill when the pad between my legs went berserk. It started to move. It kept shifting higher and higher, crawled out of my knickers and shorts and started slithering up my back. Like some nasty blood-sucking leech. During the ground jump I could feel it somewhere near my shoulder blades. As I bounced off the ground a huge stream of blood came spurting out of my swollen pussy. Sesil's coat started to turn a light pink. I was convinced it was bright red and that my blood would stain Matilda, the judges and all of the Hortobágy plain. Thoroughly flustered, I stood up to perform my last exercise, a stand on the horse without a balancing belt. I lost my balance and flopped onto the ground like a squashed plum.

Helpless, I stood next to Matilda. I felt the blood-drenched sanitary pad under my T-shirt stuck somewhere near my neck. I burst into tears. Matilda was very understanding. Nobody reproached me for anything. They assured me that coming third was also quite an achievement. To me, however, the memory of my first period was forever linked to failing at that competition. But we had a very successful vaulting season anyway. We smuggled some apple soap back from Hungary. And I got a precious Fa deodorant spray for Mum.

The medals dangling from the shelf in the living room tinkled invitingly, shimmering gold in the hot draught and forming a halo above my head. A blazing heat wave hit at the end of the summer. Sunspots drove the mercury in the thermometer up to 40° centigrade. People fainted in the street. Crows rested with their beaks wide open on a crane abandoned in the middle of our housing estate. There was tension in the air. Everything felt uncertain and nerve-wracking.

Mum plunged her swollen feet into a basin filled with ice-cold water to cool down and guzzled draft beer, repeating over and over: '*Megdöglök!* The heat's killing me!'

It was too hot to sleep at night. So we sat on the balcony nattering. Mum said she knew I would make it. Grandma would have been proud of me. We made plans for the future. We would swap our flat for a bigger one in the old town. She sat on a chair wearing her short nightie. Purple varicose veins threaded her once beautiful legs. I realised it had been ages since she had brought a boyfriend home and that she was spending more and more time in the kitchen. Her Székely goulash was the best in the world. I could never get enough of it, so she had to make it in a kettle instead of a pot.

'I'd rather dress you than feed you,' she would moan as she piled the food on my plate.

I grew like Topsy. My rapidly developing body burned calories by the million during practice. I could eat as much as I liked and remained as thin as a rake.

The vaulting season was over. Matilda gave us time off. Sesil spent whole days grazing and resting in the paddock. I have no idea what had got into Mum. She decided to throw a party at our flat, the first one in ages. All of a sudden our living room filled with neighbours. *Ein Kessel Buntes*, the East German music show was on the TV and our neighbours held glasses of vermouth as they danced to a song by Russian diva Alla Pugachova. The cheesiest music I could imagine blared out at full blast. I couldn't stand it. And I was fed up with the constant: 'Karolína, bring this, Karolína take that away, serve this, slice that, empty the ashtrays!' At last there was a brief shower of rain. The fresh air lured me out of our red-hot prefab block. I put new batteries into my Walkman and headed out.

Arpi was a magician. He had given me a Dead Can Dance cassette, warning me that it would make me shit myself. I made out the words 'The Serpent's Egg' scribbled in pencil on the cassette cover. My English wasn't very good but the woman's voice that came streaming from the headphones knocked me out. The plaintive vocals over the sound of the violin shattered my body into pieces, propelling me into the stratosphere. I became a time traveller. I found myself in another century. In another city. A bell tolled. I saw myself walking down narrow alleys somewhere in a harbour and could hear the murmur of the sea in the distance. From a church came the powerful sound of a choir singing the praises of something supernatural. People in long coats held flickering candles. A rider galloped behind my back, the horse's hooves striking the paving stones. The horse was coming closer and closer.

Suddenly someone grabbed me by the shoulder. I turned around and saw a man with a sinister smile. 'Hey, you little slut, you!' he hissed. The vodka on his breath was overwhelming. Instantly it transported me back to my drab concrete commie life. I wrenched myself free and started to run. I ran down the deserted streets of our estate with the pervert in hot pursuit. I knew I was in trouble. I could feel his hateful glance drilling a hole in my back.

I darted into a building site, a local council building-to-be, hoping to find a guard sitting in his Portakabin. But the site was silent and deserted. Huge scaffolding pierced the starless night sky. The socialist coliseum was surrounded by a metal fence. There wasn't a gap in sight, no way out. I could hear the pounding of my own pulse. My legs began to tremble. I clambered onto the scaffolding hoping that would make the pervert give up.

But he just kept coming. For a while we both crawled along like monkeys. The commies were megalomaniacs and the building was about ten stories high. At last I spotted a narrow plank, a makeshift bridge splattered with mortar. The builders had attached a towrope above it to help them get across a gaping big concrete hole safely. Without giving it a second thought I grabbed the towrope and ran over to the other side. But the window I hoped to climb into was glassed in and firmly shut. The man was about to step on the plank. I was trapped. I could feel my heart pounding in my throat. My fear stood beside me. Clammy and enormous, it trembled all over and had its arms in a twist. Its eyes, like little mirrors, reflected my bulging eyeballs.

The man took the first step. He placed a foot on the plank, holding on to the towrope with one hand. He walked slowly and carefully. He relished my helplessness. I remembered Granny's knife in my pocket and calmed down. I felt its cold handle in my palm. My fear turned into a crumpled paper handkerchief.

And then I did it. Cut!

The rope snapped and the man on the plank lost his balance. He tried to steady himself and find something to latch on to. He performed an awkward pirouette and fell into the dark depths, screaming.

Silence followed.

I stood still for a long time listening out for any rustling but heard nothing apart from the sound of a transistor radio coming from an open window.

It was 2 a.m. by the time I managed to break the damned window and set off for home. Mum was asleep on the living room floor. The bottle of vermouth was empty. The party was over. I switched off the still-buzzing TV.

I didn't tell Mum what happened that night. I didn't want to add to her worries. I locked the horrible incident away in the darkest recesses of my soul. So that dust would settle on it, so that it would decay and rot away. It was his fault anyway. He shouldn't have tried his luck with a girl descended from a hot-blooded granny. Mum slept until lunchtime and woke up with the mother of all hangovers. I inquired discreetly about her knife. Like, when was she given hers and had she ever needed to use it. She sipped the brine from a jar of pickled gherkins, clutching her forehead. 'I don't know… I must have lost it somewhere… It was just one of Granny's funny ideas anyway!'

After the weekend I went to the riding centre. It wasn't a practice day and so Romana and I lay down by a pond where we washed the horses on hot days. She laid a few linden leaves on her tummy, hoping they would leave a heart shape on her tanned skin. 'My dad died last night,' she said out of the blue.

I stiffened. I looked at her. She was totally calm. In fact, I thought I caught a glimpse of quiet joy. Who could blame her after the hell she'd been through with him. 'I'm so sorry,' I whispered and laid a yarrow blossom on her tummy.

'They found him in the garden outside our block of flats. In the rose beds. He lay there like Sleeping Beauty,' she said casually.

I heaved a sigh of relief.

Romana gave me a look: 'What's wrong?'

I told her about the previous night's pursuit and that I was wondering if the pervert who had been after me might have been her dad.

She gave a bitter laugh. 'He died of a heart attack. It wasn't him.'

I stared into Romana's green eyes and saw how strong she was.

'I can't quite imagine living without that drunk, you see,' she said. 'But we'll get by somehow. It'll be easier now that he won't be there to beat the hell out of us.'

I offered to lend her a black dress for the funeral.

In the evening I dropped by the garage to see Arpi. I hadn't seen him for a while. I returned his Dead Can Dance tape. He had lost weight and his hair was greasy and matted. He didn't feel like talking at all. There was something sad about him. He gave monosyllabic answers to my questions and when I offered him a pair of my knickers he said he wasn't interested. I didn't understand what was going on. He seemed distant, strumming on his guitar and singing some awful song.

'How about a ciggie?' I suggested, offering him one for a change.

He took the cigarette, laid down the guitar and put on something… something crazy. We sat smoking and listening. It was industrial hell. Diabolically pounding cement mixers, hydraulic presses and other kinds of machinery. With some hair-raising human screaming on top. It took me back to the building site and I saw the pervert's plummeting body.

I didn't finish my cigarette. I stood up and switched off the cassette player. 'What the hell is this?'

Apathetically exhaling smoke Arpi scratched a pimple on his face. 'This is what I'm into right now… Throbbing Gristle.'

The summer holidays were drawing to a close. Romana and I sweetened our sorrow with pistachio ice cream. It tasted like frozen parsley. A funny-looking woman in a wig was selling it from a corrugated tin shack. She reminded me of a stuffed polecat I'd seen in the natural science room at school. The first of September arrived and the teachers distributed tattered textbooks. As every year, we had to listen to the headmaster spouting drivel on the perils of imperialism, world peace and bold Young Pioneers on the school radio. The unusually strong September sun turned the classroom into a fiery furnace. We all had to squint as someone had made off with the blinds. Time dragged on unbearably. It was ages before the bell announced the end of the last class. Nothing stirred at the housing estate and the building sites were silent and empty.

The Indian summer was followed by a savage November. I would stand at the bus stop, freezing and stamping my feet. The bus was never on time. Frost drew snot from my nose. Suddenly I heard a strange noise, like a glass cracking when you pour boiling water in it. The sky turned a menacing colour. The powerful noise sounded as if a gigantic string had snapped in the sky. Stars rolled over into a new constellation and snow tumbled out of the perforated clouds. The storm began slowly and grew increasingly powerful. Sharp snowflakes pummelled the frosty ground furiously. Time started accelerating, setting people in motion. I didn't know why but I felt a fantastic sense of relief.

Mum spent all day by the receiver listening to Radio Free Europe and chain-smoking. 'This is it, my girl!' she kept repeating, showering me with kisses like crazy. 'What a shame Granny didn't live to see this.' She took the urn out of the dresser and solemnly placed it on the kitchen counter. She seemed to think Granny would hear better from there.

The 'illegal' radio station brought reports of demonstrations in Prague, of brutal police crackdowns, of people dispersed by water cannon. Students handed flowers to the cops who smashed their faces in anyway. The rallies spread like wildfire. Like night frost they stung our noses and crept under our fingernails. More and more people felt compelled to go out into the streets, to applaud and jangle their keys.

The regime was falling apart unstoppably. The headmaster gave us time off school. Mum and I wrapped up and set out for a rally carrying the national flag. Mum had tucked a flask of rum under her coat to keep warm. We stood under an improvised stage listening to dissidents giving speeches. They spoke of human rights, freedom and justice. They called on the greedy bastards to hand over power. People were in a rage. The crowd roared, vapour rising from their mouths. They looked like a herd of wild horses, ready to tear down the sturdiest fence. Every speech was welcomed by chanting. A man played the first bars of a Karel Kryl protest song. Women danced, some of the men wept and exchanged kisses. I spotted Matilda in the crowd. Mum offered her some rum. She took a big gulp, took my hand and we sang the national anthem together. Tears ran down her face. I'd never seen her so happy. Not even when we won our first medal.

The Velvet Revolution produced general euphoria. Romana and I danced on trams and traded jokes with strangers in the street. Smiles appeared, thawing faces frozen for years in grim totalitarian frowns. Our stableman vanished mysteriously and we had to take turns doing the evening feeds. That night it was my turn. I was doling out the hay. It was redolent of wild thyme and made me feel like I was holding a flowering meadow in my arms. I wanted to lie down in it. A cold moon shone behind the window like a huge shining spotlight.

The horses were munching away happily as someone entered the stables. It was a drunk crawling on the ground shouting something in German. He sounded like comrade director. Opening one box after another, he howled: *'Das Ende! Das Ende!'* I wanted to tell him to cut it out then and there unless he wanted the horses to run away and a terrible accident to happen. But there were no horses in the boxes. Instead I saw emaciated people in striped uniforms, like in concentration camp movies. The SS-man yelled. He waved a gun about and the starved prisoners stared at him with huge hungry eyes. I thought I'd lost my mind. I ran out to let the frosty air smack me back to my senses. My ears froze. My stomach trembled. I was frightened. It took me an eternity to recover. The horses went on munching their hay happily. No trace of prisoners anywhere. Only comrade director sprawled among the bales of straw, snoring loudly, a bottle of vodka in his hand.

Santa Claus arrived in December bearing the gift of the permanent collapse of communism. Mum was so elated she got plastered and burst into Hungarian songs she hadn't sung for ages. On Christmas

Eve we climbed to the top of a tower. The city's lights stretched out below us, looking just like the kitschy candles on our Christmas tree. Pale cold stars kissed the pointed cathedral spire. A firecracker went off somewhere. My fingers were numb with cold as I opened my backpack and took out the urns. Mum was laughing and weeping at the same time.

'You sure you want to do this?' I checked.

She blew her nose noisily, resolutely took the urns out of my hands and emptied them. I watched Granny's and Grandpa's ashes mingle with snowflakes and slowly fall on the ground, free at last.

We were so naïve. Especially Mum. Like a canary released from its cage, she believed that the good times were about to roll. She quit her job and started her own business. She thought we would get Granny's tavern back. She dreamt of how she would fit the place out, of the dishes she would serve and the holidays we would be able to afford on the income. She had dug out Granny's old cookery book and taught herself to cook some of the old recipes of the Austro-Hungarian monarchy. But it wasn't to be. It turned out we were not entitled to restitution. Mum had to make do with a badly-paid secretarial job, working for a former secret policeman. Everything around us was changing. Shops filled with cheap new clothes and food. A Coca-Cola advert was slapped onto the wall where Lenin's portrait used to hang. The bottle deposit cashier was replaced by a machine. Flashy foreign cars hooted their angry horns at pedestrians. Old communist-style buses now looked incongruous in the streets. Nobody landed in prison, nobody was punished for what they had done to Granny and Grandpa.

People changed their image, swapping their Communist Party membership card for a bank account. The riding centre underwent a transformation, too. Comrade director turned into a businessman. Arpi's garage was torn down to make way for a gaming parlour with blinking slot machines. Newspaper pages were full of newfangled terms such as 'market', 'competitiveness' and 'coupon privatisation'. The fine talk of freedom was drowned out by shrill TV ads. In newspaper kiosks porn magazines squeezed out the old ABC journal. We swapped our barbed wire cage for one made of gold. Everyone suddenly needed new cars, new suits and new wives. The director arrived at the riding centre in a brand new BMW. He sacked the guard and hired a skinhead, a former state security guy.

She had this way of nodding her head ever so sweetly. She was ever so graceful and grown-up. She would turn her face slowly and purr in a velvety voice: 'You can't be serious!'

Her name was Tamara.

The day before she first turned up at the riding centre I had a dream. In the dream my hair was so long that it tickled my calves. I was walking through an underpass. Crowds of people hustled and bustled around me, pushing and shoving me every which way. I stepped onto an escalator and realised with horror that my hair had got caught in the steps. I tried to pull it out. I pulled and pulled as if my life depended on it. My panic grew as I got closer to the place where the stairs disappeared. The escalator teeth were dragging me inside. I screamed. My head hurt. I could see the escalator scalping me. I clutched my bloodied skull. The crowd was roaring away and pushing me. Nobody did anything to stop the escalator. Mum woke me up. My whole body was shaking. For the first time in ages she let me climb into her bed.

And the next day *she* appeared.

I was in the middle of doing the mill on Cecil's back when, from the corner of my eye, I registered a small figure. Her black hair emphasised the china-doll whiteness of her skin. She fixed me with her gaze and smiled. Her light blue eyes — rimmed by amazing thick eyelashes — looked like icy holes. Cold and distant. They didn't betray the slightest trace of the smile on her lips. Her gaze unnerved me. It rocked me. It threw me off balance. I fell off and tumbled to the ground. I hadn't fallen like that for a very long time. My fall was a sign of the things to come.

Everyone was enchanted with Tamara. Especially Matilda. The new girl was so polished. So talented, always bursting with great ideas. She was the only one who managed to do a handstand at a canter. She took an instant dislike to Romana and me. She had no sense of humour and took offence at Romana's kindhearted teasing. She was full of herself and believed she always knew best. For example, when lunging Sesil she wanted to show off how obedient he was. She took a carrot and told the horse to ask for it. She patted his leg with a whip and repeated: 'Ask, ask!' Sesil didn't care about the carrot and ground his teeth, irritated by the whip. 'This horse is stupid,' she declared. She gave the lunge line to Romana so she could lead him back to the box.

Romana smiled. She scratched Sesil behind the ear and took out a sugar cube. 'Leg, Sesil dear, give us your hoof, please,' she asked nicely. Sesil gave her his leg several times and took the sugar.

Tamara turned pale. She threw Romana the most hateful glance I have ever seen. She never forgave her.

Once I accidentally left a slice of bread with jam on her chair and Tamara sat on it. A black spot appeared on her designer tracksuit bottoms that everyone envied, smack on her bum. Someone yelled that she had shat herself. From then on it was all-out war. Tamara never spoke to us again. We were training for competitions that were to decide whether we would advance to the European championship. We started working really hard, with a schedule that meant practising twice a day.

At school we were excused from class. Matilda knew the right people in the right places. She organised a free gym where we could practise on a pommel horse. She knew a gymnastic coach who helped us master complicated acrobatic moves.

'We must turn professional,' Matilda declared. 'Our performance must improve if we want to survive. Nobody is going to give us anything for free, we've got to keep winning!'

Trick riding suddenly stopped being just for fun. We started to slave away and learned to be competitive. Failure at competitions was not an option. Matilda went on and on about flawless performances and perseverance. She got rid of our little red skirts and replaced them with trendy new sports outfits that squeezed our young bodies painfully. Before we knew it we were caught in the rivalry trap. Matilda no longer sang our praises. At the end of practice she would often criticise us. She made us try dangerous, scary moves. It was all easy-peasy for Tamara, who flew from one acrobatic trick to the next with the greatest of ease. Her body seemed to be made of rubber. She flitted in front of us so fast it gave me nausea.

'Follow her example,' shouted Matilda, devouring Tamara with her eyes as she swung off the horse in a double back somersault. 'You've got to understand that competition at this level will be really tough. No more little girls having fun on their little horsies. Starting tomorrow I'll be timing you. Each of you must finish your freestyles inside one minute. No mistakes or hesitation. Do we understand each other?'

The sound of her voice felt like the lashing of a whip. She stopped asking how we were. We no longer sat around on haystacks after training. We no longer discussed our problems or planned our future. Matilda and Tamara would lock themselves in the coaches' office for secret confabs. They clearly had some serious things to discuss. Without us. The constant slaving away at the gym and on the horse began to take its toll on me. I started falling asleep in the middle of dinner with my head on the table. Mum had great difficulty dragging me to bed. But even worse than the exhaustion was the weird atmosphere that suddenly reigned in our team. We all noticed that Matilda had fallen under Tamara's spell. Some girls started to suck up to her. Provocative and biting comments became routine as the girls tried to ingratiate themselves with Tamara. Many took to imitating her, others tried to flatter her. It was disgusting.

'Hard choices will have to made,' Matilda announced one day. 'Only those riders who get a minimum of ten, nine or eight points will take part in the competition. Every mistake means a point taken off. You get zero points if you leave out a move. And remember, you're being timed!'

There was grumbling in the group.

'And who will be awarding the points?' asked Romana as she put on her trainers.

'Why, Tamara and me, of course,' said Matilda, her eyes flashing. I noticed an eerie change about the queen inside her. Her eyes glowed fiercely, her pupils were dilated and there were pearls of perspiration on her face. She looked feverish.

'Our queen has picked up some kind of infectious disease,' I whispered into Romana's ear. She stood beside me, staring silently into the queen's crazed eyes. She seemed mesmerised. We were all on edge. All of us. Except for Tamara. She was leaning casually against the riding hall wall, her arms folded across her chest. Her cruel empty eyes made me shudder. I gave it my all and performed as if my life depended on it. I pointed my toes so hard I almost got cramp. Sweat poured down my face, forming salt crystals in my hair as it dried.

Romana pushed herself to the limit. When she did the mill she seemed to be flying through the air. While she was performing a stand at a canter, Sesil stumbled. Because of her unequal legs she couldn't regain her balance. She scrambled back to her feet with tears in her eyes. The girls watched her limp back to the changing rooms. A menacing silence descended. Romana looked like a lame bird that had been shot.

'It was the horse that stumbled,' I said, trying to salvage what I could of the situation.

Matilda pressed her lips together cruelly. Tamara ran up to her and whispered something in her ear. Matilda gave her a smile and said: 'Let's carry on!'

We didn't make it. Romana had fallen off and I had gone over time. We had the lowest score and ended up as substitutes. Maids-of-all-work. Put this away, bring that, tidy up this, clean that up, hand walk the horse, muck out! Matilda focused on the future contestants and we never got to ride. During practice we would just sit in the riding hall watching as the other girls went through the drill. Almost unnoticeably, resentment grew inside us.

'We've been brushed aside for good,' Romana fumed. 'We've been thrown on the rubbish heap!'

We were leading a worn-out Sesil to the stables. He was out of breath and slightly lame. Matilda sternly instructed us to wipe him dry and dress his hooves properly. Not like the last time.

Romana got mad. With arms akimbo, she said: 'What are you on about?' Matilda fluttered her eyelids. 'The last time you didn't put oil on Cecil's hooves!'

'Of course we couldn't, as her majesty now kept the oil locked away in the office,' Romana retorted.

And I sneered: 'Don't think we're going to spend our own money on hoof oil. You're the coach, it's your job to get supplies from the boss!'

All hell broke loose. Matilda's face turned crimson. Her eyes blazed with fury. 'Who the hell do you think you are? You cheeky little shits!' she yelled.

Tamara came running over and put her arm around her shoulder. 'Calm down,' she said, trying to pacify her, 'these two aren't worth it!'

Matilda's bullying got steadily worse. She would find fault with everything we did. When we got Sesil's coat all gleaming, she claimed his tail hadn't been combed properly. If his tail had been combed she got mad at us for not treating the bridle. She would always find something to complain about. And we, in turn, were a right pain in the neck. We talked back. Before practice we exercised on a stationary Sesil without HER permission. We were in open rebellion. We undermined Matilda's authority and questioned her decisions, which drove her absolutely mad. And we were careless. We would lead Sesil from the paddock straight into practice. We stopped and chatted by the gate and let the silly creature wallow in the mud until he turned all black. We had to give him another shower and wait for him to dry off. The practice session had to be cancelled.

'You did that on purpose,' Matilda fumed and said we were now barred from taking part in the demo performance as well. Things were obviously getting serious. The big showdown was coming. And all the signs were that Romana and I were on the losing side. We just couldn't imagine not being part of the demo. Even though we'd been relegated to substitutes we wouldn't for the world miss the wonderful experience of trick riding in front of an audience. We swallowed our pride and let it deflate like a balloon although we still pretended not to care. Eventually we relented and decided to try and bury the hatchet.

We knocked on the door of Matilda's office and waited like good girls.

'Come in,' Tamara called out.

We took a deep breath and walked in. Matilda was in her underwear. I couldn't take my eyes off her beautiful trim body. She was putting her tights on and when she noticed my stare she quickly pulled on a jumper. Tamara was sitting in an armchair, reading a magazine. She pretended we weren't there.

'Matilda, we're sick and tired of fighting you. Let's put it all behind us. We would really like things to be the way they used to be between us. Please do let us perform at the demo. It means the world to us.' The words came tumbling out of Romana.

Matilda slowly straightened up and I smelled the old familiar fragrance again. She looked into Romana's eyes intently, then turned to me. For a brief moment I thought I saw her noble queen inside her, ready to hear out her equestrienne. But only for a moment, because the second she opened her mouth to speak Tamara's velvety voice chimed in: 'But didn't you say that the whole point of the demo was to attract sponsors? They're only interested in the competition team.' The queen's face contorted, her lips twisting in a disdainful grimace. She closed her eyes and the ruby-red apples in her mouth began to rot.

I took a deep breath: 'We too are... part of the team.' Matilda turned her tights the right way out and hissed with sheer hatred: 'No! You two are the team wreckers!'

I couldn't tell who or what was inside Tamara. Every time I took a better look at her, all I could see was a bottomless ice pit. The ice came pouring out of her eyes freezing everything it touched. Including Matilda's heart. Romana's inner warrior sharpened her spear and emitted a war cry. I knew this wasn't going to end well. And when I saw a new vaulting horse in the hall I realised it was all over for Sesil as well. They replaced him with a splendid black horse with white socks. At a canter, he showed off his high-stepping. He was younger and more presentable. Compared to him Sesil was a has-been.

Romana and I started spending time in the hayloft again. 'We can't give up, Karolína, we've got to fight,' she said, all worked up. 'They have no right to push us aside like this! We should start our own vaulting team!'

I didn't say a word but agreed with everything she said. My throat tensed up with anxiety.

I watched the swallows return to their nests as they did each year. An unwieldy forklift truck whirred in the yard, shifting bales of straw. Builders used jackhammers to tear down the walls of what had been the tackroom. It was going to be turned into garages. I realised that the carefree times at the riding centre were gone forever. A white Toyota pulled up below the stable windows and hooted twice. A woman in garish make-up and tight jodhpurs climbed out. She cracked a small whip on her shiny riding boots. The director crawled out of his office. He had visibly put on weight. A breeze lifted the inept comb-over off his expanding bald spot. The woman in jodhpurs smiled and he smiled back. 'Hello, young lady, we've got our finest horse waiting for you,' he said, kissing her hand. The car gave two beeps and the director and the woman vanished in the stables.

The place underwent a swift and spectacular transformation.

Membership fees went up a thousand per cent. Horses were now available for hire. They would come and go, like on an assembly line. The director obtained a licence to run a fancy bar. Those who could afford it could relax in a sauna after riding. The riding hall was plastered with adverts. A girl in a swim suit stood by the wall washing a Mercedes. Rumour had it that the director had bought the newly privatised riding centre for peanuts. He hired Matilda as a professional coach. She had to give riding lessons to children of the nouveaux riches. She went out for lunches with him. He paid her a very decent salary, and Matilda's revulsion for the former comrade vanished for good. She became a loyal employee and slave-driver of her subordinates. I couldn't believe my eyes. All those who couldn't stand the director before were now licking his arse. Just so they wouldn't lose their jobs. Romana and I prepared to mount our last attack. As Granny used to say: 'If you've got to go, go out with a bang.'

On the day of the demo performance we led Sesil out of the paddock to a nearby meadow. Tables groaning with refreshments had been laid out by the course track. Businessmen sipped their whiskies. Everyone was having a great time. A loudspeaker announced the trick riding team that would represent Equus Ltd. at the European championships. There was a modest ripple of applause. Techno music boomed from the loudspeakers. Matilda cracked her whip. The young riders gave a bow.

Tamara was the first to mount a horse. Romana and I burst into the arena with a spruced-up Sesil and performed our own show alongside the representation team. I led the horse on the lunge while Romana rode in her white trainers and little red skirt. We performed one trick after another. Her show to the techno beat was like a speeded-up film. She pretended she was scared. From time to time she would fall off on purpose. Then she would vault on again with an exaggerated limp. She looked like a crippled circus clown. The businessmen roared with laughter. They had eyes only for the two of us. Matilda began to pant helplessly. Tamara looked paler than usual on her black horse. Then Romana and I switched places. I leapt onto Sesil and time slowed down. With pointed feet I raised my legs as slowly as I could. The move lasted an eternity. The spectators saw every tilt of my body, every movement of my arms, in slow motion. Sometimes I would repeat a move, as if someone were fiddling with a remote control. When I finished my star trick, the slowest ground jump in the world, someone whistled. I revelled in my success, proud of my vaulting skills. We bowed to the audience. We got a standing ovation. I saw outrage on the director's face and felt Matilda's furious glance drilling into my back. The demo was over. After that nobody would speak to us. Not even the toilet lid. We ceased to exist. Our former friends looked through us. Nobody would even acknowledge our greeting. We were dangerous bitches, disruptive females who disregarded all the rules. The director summoned us for a dressing down.

He was sitting in a leather armchair holding a drink. 'You have violated the ban, exposed the coach to ridicule and brought Sesil out without permission. Sesil is owned by MY business. You broke safety regulations and seriously damaged the reputation of this riding establishment,' he shouted. We should have been grateful that we'd been allowed to muck out manure. If we didn't come to our senses, he would kick us out, regardless of our past contribution and achievements. Blah-blah-blah. Romana squared up to him proud and ramrod-straight with defiance in her eyes.

'But the audience had a great time, didn't they?' I said, trying to present our circus show in a more favourable light.

The director gave me a bemused look. 'That's the only reason you're still here. Otherwise you'd be out of the door this minute.'

Fortunately, the phone rang just at that moment and we made ourselves scarce. I wondered aloud why the SS-man inside the director had an olive-coloured emerald where his left eye should have been.

Romana shouted me down. 'Karolína, I really couldn't give a shit about your visions right now!'

I took her hand and led her to the changing rooms. I opened a Milan Assortment packet, and when she calmed down we went off to groom Sesil.

I found Mum sitting in the kitchen with the fridge door open wide. 'Defrosting the fridge, are you?' I asked but she just slapped the fridge door with a cloth and frowned at me. Oh, she's in one of her moods, I thought and hoped I could make a quick getaway.

'How about doing your share of the chores for once?' she said, having a go at me. 'You just mooch around doing nothing all day long and let me slave away! And those T-shirts of yours, I washed them a week ago and they're still on your desk where I left them! Doesn't it bother you they're getting covered in dust?'

I didn't respond. It was best to keep quiet when Mum was in one of her moods, let her swear and shout and get it out of her system.

'*Ez a kurva élet,* this fucking life!' she shouted, and I noticed that her nail varnish had peeled off.

She looked rather the worse for wear. I suspected she'd had a bit to drink. 'And those shoes I bought you a month ago, they're ruined! Do you think I'm made of money?'

I knew she was about to reach boiling point. I sat down and braced myself for a torrent of reproach.

'We can't go on like this, Karolína! Everything is too bloody expensive and I don't earn enough to keep paying for this fancy sport of yours! The windcheater I got you last year stinks of manure and the sleeves are all torn!' she screamed, slapping the wet cloth down on the floor.

I tried to explain that it was Sesil who had accidentally ripped the windcheater with his teeth by mistake during some innocent horseplay but she wouldn't let me get a word in.

'I've had fucking enough!' she said in a smooth transition from shouting to weeping. 'You're an ungrateful, lazy little bitch!' Her face was streaked with black mascara. She looked like a desperate alcoholic.

I reached for the cloth and said I would finish the cleaning. She should go and watch a film on TV. Mum was sobbing. She hated having to go to the cheap Vietnamese shops. But there was no way she could make more money. She took an open bottle of wine from the cupboard. I poured her a glass.

'Romana and I have been kicked off the team,' I informed her laconically as I started to clean the fridge.

Mum didn't seem to take it in. She took a sip of wine, then burst into tears again. 'But you were supposed to compete, weren't you? What did you get up to, huh? All that money that I have put into that trick riding of yours! And you end up getting yourself kicked off!'

As I scratched bits of dried egg off the fridge I tried to explain what had happened at the riding centre. She wasn't listening. She went on and on about how much of her money and nerves she had put into it.

'So what. I'll go and get a job. I'll help you around the house and I'll dye your hair too, you're looking like an old woman,' I said, trying to lighten things up a bit. 'Besides, I'm going to sit the college entrance exams soon, so at least I'll have time to work.'

The thought of the money I could earn if I got a job helped to dry Mum's tears. 'But who will take on a slip of a girl like you?' she said doubtfully.

I went on scrubbing the fridge. 'But I'm sixteen already, Mum!' I couldn't stand it when she treated me like a little kid!

She had some more wine. Then she sighed and went to phone her friend Gizka to ask if she knew of a job for me.

Soon enough I was delivering papers. Getting used to a 4 a.m. start nearly killed me. But later I came to love that time of the day, when the city is slowly waking up. The streets were empty and quiet. They belonged to the feral cats who prowled around, throttling any young birds that had fallen out of their nests. Car engines were not yet humming and nothing disturbed the dawn chorus of the robins and the aroma of freshly baked bread.

The work itself was undemanding, though I had to walk miles. I didn't mind being fobbed off with the farthest end of our estate where the older delivery women refused to go. I was still quite fit. I would listen to the morning conversations drifting out of open windows and to party music still droning on after everyone had gone to sleep. I enjoyed it all. Sometimes I would browse through magazines we couldn't get under communism, like *National Geographic* or *Koktejl*, its Czech counterpart. I found an article about a man who lived with hyenas. He talked to them, too. One photo showed him feeding a hyena raw meat, mouth-to-mouth.

One day, a Friday morning like any other, I sat down on the stairs at the entrance to a block of flats to read the latest issue of *Koktejl* when I spotted someone lying below the stairs. A drunk, I thought. I glanced at his feet. There was something familiar about them. I put the magazines back in the cart and walked down to him. I saw syringes, used needles, bottles and bits of cardboard scattered on the ground and there, among them…

'Arpi!' I exclaimed in amazement.

He didn't respond. I touched him to check he was alive. He was filthy and emaciated. The pimples on his face shone bright like a red traffic lights.

'Oh, it's you,' he said, stirring. 'Thought it was the cops.'

I helped him get to his feet. He was as light as a feather. Or crumpled paper. He was shivering. 'Give us a twenty!' he begged.

His eyes were strange and glassy. He reminded me of an angry animal. I offered him a salami roll.

'I'm not hungry, I just need to buy something.'

I didn't know what he meant.

We stared at each other as if we'd never met before. He smiled and I noticed his teeth were chipped.

'Will you play me something on your guitar?' I asked.

Arpi said he had sold it, he'd found something that was a million times better than the guitar! Something that helped him compose the most brilliant songs in his head.

'Oh yeah, and I'm Jitka Zelenková' I replied sarcastically. At the thought of the ageing Czech pop star it suddenly all clicked. I picked up my cart and wanted to press on.

'But we're pals, aren't we?' he said, hopping before me and taking my hand. 'Who bought you chocolates at the supermarket? And what about the great music I used to give you… and all the cigs?'

I stared at his dirty fingernails and fingers stained yellow with tobacco. His whole body was shaking. The magic eyes of the Egyptian priest were gone. He reminded me of the abused dog I had just read about. Without a word I took some money out of my pocket. Arpi snatched it from my hand and vanished among the high-rises.

Mum started to giggle in a funny way. At first I thought it was because of my job until I found some pills in her handbag. I asked what that was supposed to mean. She just grunted that I should stop telling her what to do. She claimed she was under constant pressure to smile and be in a pleasant mood. She had to work late and it was all getting too much.

I wanted to do my bit, so I started to do the cooking. My first awful attempts were inedible but gradually I learned to prepare a few dishes. Noodles with cabbage, bean soup, pumpkin sauce. I made the same dishes over and over again.

One day I invited Romana over for lunch. She didn't like my cabbage noodles. Too spicy, she said. She was better off since her dad had died. Her mum inherited some land. She bought Romana special shoes that almost completely disguised her limp. She wore make-up and nice clothes. She looked like a girl from a good family. She had started college and was going to become a make-up artist. She clearly enjoyed it. Next to her I looked like a commie throwback.

We spent less and less time at the riding centre now. Romana was too busy and I was too poor. Once a week we would muck out and take Sesil for a walk in the woods. Nobody rode him anymore. I knew his days were numbered. But I would have never dreamt that they would get rid of him in such a callous way.

We found him in a paddock jam-packed with horses, staring at the stables. Some were biting each other's backs. A shiny padlock hung on the gate. The woods were ablaze with the colours of autumn. The air smelled of mushrooms. I remember the sparkling cobwebs scattered about tree branches. They reminded me of the lace curtains in Juci *néni's* room.

The stableman tersely informed us that the horses in the paddock were waiting for slaughter. Romana and I stroked Sesil's muzzle. He begged for carrots. I imagined him crammed into some stinking lorry and trampled by other terrified horses. I pictured people beating him to make him shuffle over to the deadly box where he would get stunned with the electric current and have his head chopped off. Feeling utterly helpless, I burst into tears The thought that OUR Sesil would be ground into salami and his hooves turned into gelatine drove me into a frenzy.

'We just can't let them do it,' I sobbed.

I felt Romana shivering. Her make-up, dissolved by her tears, flowed down her face. She was biting her lips trying to come up with something sensible. 'We'll come at night and... steal him!' she said, glancing at me. She was pale.

'A horse is not a matchbox,' I pointed out.

She wiped off her make-up and smeared Sesil's throat with her dirty hand.

I lit up. The cigarette calmed me down and I was able to compose myself. 'There's only one way.'

Romana said nothing. She knew what I meant. She turned even paler. She looked like the grim reaper with black blotches for eyes.

I stroked her cheek. A strange calm came over me.

'We haven't got much time. They'll take them away tomorrow,' she whispered. I stubbed out the ciggie, took Romana's hand and off we went into the woods. To find something that would set Sesil free.

We walked in total silence. Gusts of wind tore the coloured leaves off the trees. They floated down like wedding confetti. I tried to remember where I had seen the tree we needed. It took us an hour to find it. It grew in the middle of a small clearing where we had lain in the sun so many times. *Taxus baccata.* A lovely name, isn't it? It sounds like an incantation from Saxana, the teenage witch from the Czech film. It's a charming little evergreen, the yew. And highly poisonous. The wolf on my pocketknife bared its sinister teeth. The sharp blade bit into the fragrant bark.

Back home we chopped the needles into tiny pieces and stuffed them into apples and dry rolls. Romana was crying. Her green eyes shed lakes of horror-filled tears. 'I'm not coming with you,' she said. She gave me a bear hug. The warrior within her bowed her head and laid down her arms.

I waited for darkness to fall and the skinhead security guy to disappear inside his cabin. He put on a video. The chirping of a lone cricket mingled with the moaning of a porn actress coming from the open window. I turned into a silent black shadow and dashed past the locked stables, brushing against the sleeping German shepherd. I stopped at the gates of the paddock where they kept the horses condemned to death. The horses were silent. Sesil was the only one happy to see me. He stuck his head into the canvas backpack greedily. The whole thing took less than twenty minutes. His teeth chattered, he staggered and collapsed to the ground. His eyes rolled back. He began to foam at the mouth, then came a few death rattles. The herd snorted nervously, forming a circle around their dying mate. I stroked his head. The moon popped out from behind a cloud and cast its light over the nearby meadow as Sesil's turquoise soul galloped off into eternity.

It took me a long time to realise that I had reached the end of the road. I've always been a bit slow on the uptake. The most successful years of my life were the ones under the totalitarian regime. How ironic. I felt like a collaborator. My best memories related to a time you're not supposed to have anything good to say about. I had reached the peak just once, my star had flared for a moment and then fizzled out. Tough luck, girl! The mountain summit turned into a sand dune, into which my feet started to sink. I sank lower and lower. Maybe I should have killed myself on that day the equestrienne inside me was truly happy. I should have come home from the competition, taken a bath and put on some nice clothes. I should have gone to bed, spread my glittering prizes around me, and swallowed some pills or turned on the gas. That's what I should have done. Except that I didn't. And so I had to watch the Egyptian priest dig his own grave. The only things he left behind were a few white pebbles in the sand. I had to watch helplessly as the Indian princess dissolved in a glass of wine. Only a golden earring was left at the bottom. I saw the warrior break her spear. She turned into a doll with lipstick-red lips. My eye trick no longer worked. I saw only endless grey fog drifting around me. My knife had gone rusty. The emptiness made me go dead inside. The equestrienne turned into an empty vessel. Hollow, like a pumpkin. If someone patted her on the back, she would make a strange echoing sound. But I have gone on living and survived hundreds of thousands of mornings and millions of nights. I have grown old, my face has become wrinkled. For years I've been musing about the best way to do it. And I waited. Waited and waited. Until I started to reek of urine. Until someone high above my head finally watered the geraniums with a sprinkler and a bad-tempered grey horse galloped onto the meadow. I let my mouth fill with saliva so that I could let off a proper volley of spit in his face. Silvery spider-webs floated in the air. The world suddenly seemed wonderfully distant. The old squaw pressed her lips to mine and her long kiss erased the last remaining memory from my mind.

Acknowledgements

The translators would like to thank Lucy Popescu for her insightful comments on an earlier draft.

PARTHIAN TRANSLATIONS

EXILES

Dónall Mac Amhlaigh

Translated from Irish
by Mícheál Ó hAodha

Out October 2020

£12.00
978-1-912681-31-0

HANA

Alena Mornštajnová

Translated from Czech
by Julia and Peter Sherwood

Out October 2020

£10.99
978-1-912681-50-1

LA BLANCHE

Maï-Do Hamisultane

Translated from French
by Suzy Ceulan Hughes

£8.99
978-1-912681-23-5

THE NIGHT CIRCUS AND OTHER STORIES

Uršuľa Kovalyk

Translated from Slovak
by Julia and Peter Sherwood

£8.99
978-1-912681-04-4

A GLASS EYE

Miren Agur Meabe

Translated from Basque
by Amaia Gabantxo

£8.99
978-1-912109-54-8

HER MOTHER'S HANDS

Karmele Jaio

Translated from Basque
by Kristin Addis

£8.99
978-1-912109-55-5

WOMEN WHO BLOW ON KNOTS

Ece Temelkuran

Translated from Turkish
by Alexander Dawe

£9.99
978-1-910901-69-4

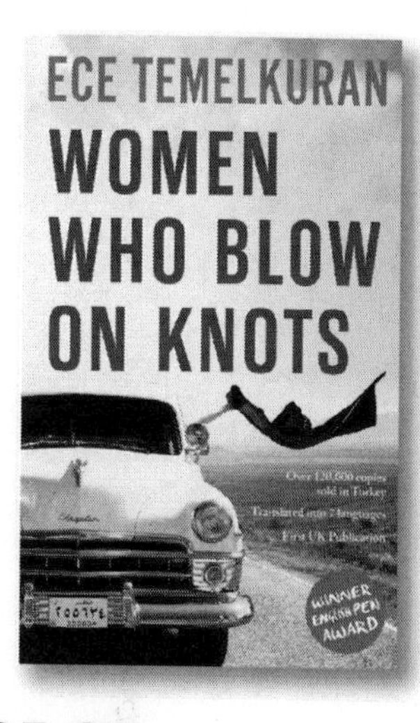

THE HOUSE OF THE DEAF MAN

Peter Krištúfek

Translated from Slovak
by Julia and Peter Sherwood

£11.99
978-1-909844-27-8

PARTHIAN TRANSLATIONS

DEATH DRIVES AN AUDI

Kristian Bang Foss

Winner of the European Prize for Literature

£10.00
978-1-912681-32-7

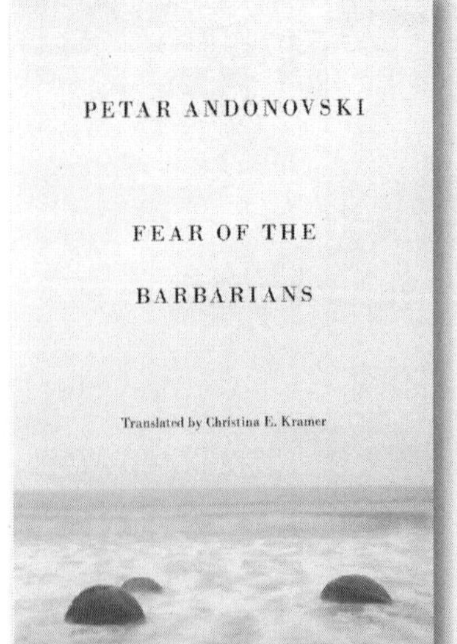

FEAR OF BARBARIANS

Petar Adonovski

Winner of the European Prize for Literature

£9.00
978-1-913640-19-4